DEADLY WARNING

"You know, Slocum," the rider said, "that's a pretty little girl, that Amanda. 'Course, I like a woman with a little meat on her bones, know what I mean? But some of them boys got different ideas." He laughed.

Slocum grabbed the man by the wrist and pulled him down until their faces were mere inches apart. "I'm warning you, mister, I find so much as a smear of dirt on that girl's cheek and you're a dead man. You understand me?" He twisted until something snapped in the rider's wrist, then flung the arm away like a butcher ridding himself of a chicken head.

"You son of a bitch . . ."

"Save it," Slocum snapped.

OTHER BOOKS BY JAKE LOGAN

JAKE LOGAN

SLOW DEATH

BERKLEY BOOKS, NEW YORK

SLOW DEATH

A Berkley Book / published by arrangement with
the author

PRINTING HISTORY
Berkley edition / July 1989

ISBN: 0-425-11649-2

A BERKLEY BOOK ® TM 757,375
Berkley Books are published by The Berkley Publishing Group
200 Madison Avenue, New York, N.Y. 10016.
The name "BERKLEY" and the "B" logo
are trademarks belonging to Berkley Publishing Corporation.

PRINTED IN THE UNITED STATES OF AMERICA

10 9 8 7 6 5 4 3 2 1

1

John Slocum watched the sun rise over the mountains. The brightening red disc, bloody at first, then thinning to orange and finally turning yellow, climbed up behind the Little Belt Range. As the sun rose higher, he sipped his coffee, conscious of the Rockies behind him. It was an odd sensation. He felt as if he were perched on the tongue of some giant beast, the ragged teeth of two mountain ranges beginning to close in on him like the jaws of a cougar.

The Rockies were already alive with gold and oranges, yellow and bright browns, as the fall started its last month. Sitting on his haunches, he felt as if something were about to end for him. Not just a season, but a chapter in his life, maybe even more than that.

It was peaceful here, and he hadn't seen another soul in nearly a week. But some things had to be acknowledged. He was down to his last few dollars, and he had few prospects. Running through the names of people he knew in Montana, people who wouldn't mind seeing him again anyway, he realized he didn't need to take off his boots to count them all. With winter coming, he knew he'd better find some work, something to carry him through until spring. As beautiful as the mountains were, they could be even more cruel. Prospects and a respect for the beautiful wouldn't keep him warm when the snows came.

He downed the last of his coffee and got up slowly, his

joints stiff and creaking a little. He stiff-legged it to the campfire and squatted down to pour himself another cup. The trout, a big brown beauty, was flaky and white, just about done. He shook the small frying pan, making sure the fish hadn't stuck to the metal, then flipped the trout over and set the pan to one side. The pan was hot enough to finish the cooking.

The coffee was strong and black. He'd run out of sugar two weeks before, and he never used milk, even when he could get it. Absently, he swirled the bitter brown liquid in his mouth, then let it slide down his throat, feeling its heat burn all the way down to his gut. His horse whinnied, getting a little restless after a night on a hobble.

"Hold on, hold on," Slocum said. "You're worse than a woman. Never satisfied." The horse shuffled impatiently but made no more noise. Slocum laughed to himself and then washed the laugh down with another swallow of the scalding coffee. He set the cup on a flat rock, shoved the rock in toward the flames to keep the coffee warm, then grabbed the frying pan. Using the flat edge of his knife, he broke the fish in bite-size pieces, watching for bones as he shoved each piece to one side of the pan. Spearing a piece on the point of his blade, he chewed it three or four times, then swallowed. The fish was done to a turn, the meat moist and delicious.

Slocum wolfed down the rest of his meal, keeping one eye on the sky. He had a long way to go, and he was already three days late. Jake Farrell had a job waiting for him, but, like most things people needed, it wouldn't keep for very long. Farrell was a friend, but even friends had their limits. Slocum didn't want to push his luck.

When the food was gone, he cleaned his gear and packed it into his saddlebags. He shook out his bedroll, then curled it into a taut tube and strapped it to the back of his saddle. The broad, wide brook, full of cold, clear water from the mountains, gurgled a few yards away, and Slocum filled his canteens, then draped them over his saddle horn.

He poured water on the fire, then kicked the wet ashes into a thin paste, stomping them into the earth to make sure they were out. It hadn't rained for a few days, and the grass wouldn't take much to set it afire. The big horse, anxious to get moving, snuffed restlessly, trying to shake off the rawhide hobble binding its ankles.

Slocum undid the hobble, then climbed into the saddle. He turned to look over his shoulder at the broad rolling country stretching away to the east, the horizon barely concealing the low Little Belt Mountains to the east. To the west, the more ominous Rockies, their ragged edge jutting into the endless blue sky, formed a backdrop for his invisible destination. He felt again, for a moment, like a choice morsel on the tongue of a ravenous beast whose restless jaws were poised just before closing down to tear him to shreds.

They called it the Big Sky Country, and, looking up into the endless blue, he understood why. The sensation was dizzying. For a few seconds he lost his sense of direction. It felt as if he were leaning over the mouth of a deep, indigo well, on the verge of falling in. This was a country that could swallow you whole, one way or another. There wouldn't be bones to mark your passing, and not a ripple on the watery sky to betray your disappearance.

Slocum remembered the night before. Lying in the bedroll, his eyes half closed against the sharp points of the stars, he wondered how he had come to be here. The howling of wolves, closer than he liked, though not near as close as he feared, kept reminding him how insignificant he was, how much a stranger he was here.

John Slocum was a man used to being alone, but that didn't mean he liked it. There were ways to be free without wandering rootless and unknown across the map, drifting into towns he'd never seen before, and out again before more than half a dozen people even realized he'd been there. It wasn't a choice, not really. It was a condition.

There had been something else for him, a long time ago, some other possibility. But standing in a ragged file at Chancellorsville, friends on both sides of him slowly torn to pieces by the incessant musket fire, everything had changed. He had been melted down in that crucible, and recast. Whatever he had been died with his friends. What he was to become, he didn't know then, and wondered whether he did yet.

What he remembered most was the smell. Blood, thick and sweet in the air, the overripe stench of voided bowels and the sharp tang of gunsmoke. Wrapped in clouds of it, he had wandered like a deaf-mute, feeling his way with the end of his own gun, like a blind man with a heavy stick. He had been fighting for something, he knew that, and he kept reminding himself of it.

What he could not know was that there were others, men he knew, men his family had trusted, who didn't care what he had been fighting for. What mattered to them was that he was gone, and the family defenseless. He had come home after the war to find everything changed. The family holdings were no longer his to share. The family itself was gone. And for John Slocum, there had been only the sound of a spade in damp earth as he buried those who had betrayed him, and the sharp snap of the flames as they devoured everything that had once been his. With nothing left for him there in Georgia, nothing beyond the heap of ashes and the mound of damp earth, he had ridden away.

He still hadn't looked back. There was no reason to. He knew, as sure as he knew the smell of blood, that everything that had been his was gone. Mounting up and riding away had taken only a few seconds, perhaps less. And yet, it was the most difficult thing he had ever had to do. In the ten thousand mountings since then, he had seen the painful echo of that small gesture. Still, out of habit, he stared at the earth as if to memorize, some hidden part of him knowing that he would never see that particular plot of land again.

So it had come to this. A possible job in a distant place. It wasn't much to live for, but it was all he had. Turning his back on the trail behind him, Slocum stared into the western mountains, his long shadow stretching out ahead of him almost to the edge of the world.

He needed a few supplies, and he hoped to get them in the next day or so. If he could run across a trail, he could get some salt and flour, buy a little gunpowder for the Colt Navy that slapped against his thigh as he rode. The big stallion seemed to sense his mood, breaking into a trot as soon as the spurs nicked its flanks.

The thick sod, dry now with the lack of rain, cushioned the stallion's hooves. An hour's ride brought him to a dusty gash in the yellow-green grass. It wasn't the deeply rutted road gouged by the thousands of wagons that had passed through on the way to the Pacific Northwest. More likely it was one of those natural routes scraped by wranglers in threes and fives, moving from job to job and place to place, or maybe even the wagon track of small landowners passing to and from a small town.

The small clouds of dust kicked up by the stallion's hooves formed a narrow, thin tube behind him. He could look back over his shoulder and see where he'd been. He still had no real idea where he was going. He searched the horizon ahead for some sign of life. He hadn't seen a soul in nearly a week, and so far there was no evidence that this part of the world was inhabited. It was a cold morning; maybe a column of smoke from a late fire would signal a settlement, a ranch, or a farm.

The big stallion stumbled suddenly. Slocum sawed the

reins, trying to rescue the animal from a misstep. The horse limped a few paces, and Slocum yanked his boots free of the stirrups. The horse pitched forward as Slocum leaped free, then rolled onto its side.

Slocum scrambled to his feet as the horse struggled. It whinnied, getting to its knees. As it tried to rise again, it crumpled and fell over. This time it lay on its side, panting heavily. Slocum ran to the horse, hoping it wasn't as bad as it looked. In the middle of nowhere, the animal was his only link with something even passing for civilization.

He dropped to one knee and examined the horse. Carefully feeling each foreleg from hoof to knee, he found what he was looking for on the second. The sharp edge of broken bone, nearly through the skin, was the worst possible evidence. There was no way the horse could walk, even without him on its back.

Slocum patted the big stallion on its muzzle, then loosened the cinch. He tugged the saddle free, then removed the reins. The bit dangled loosely, a small hunk of bright metal in the cool air. The horse seemed to watch it, as if it were some insect he had never seen before. The big brown eyes looked at Slocum for a second, then followed the bit as Slocum hurled the reins away in disgust.

Taking a deep breath, Slocum patted the animal again, talking to it in a soft voice. He pulled the Colt Navy from his holster and stood up. He backed away slowly, the horse still watching him. Its eyes were motionless, as if the animal were waiting for something to happen. Slocum aimed deliberately, then closed his eyes as he squeezed the trigger.

The report of the heavy pistol sounded like thunder in the empty sky. The horse whinnied once then was silent. As Slocum opened his eyes again, the animal was still twitching slightly, its legs jerking in a final spasm. Then it lay still.

Slowly, Slocum stepped closer to the dead horse. His eyes, as if with a will of their own, stared at the gaping hole in the animal's skull. A pool of bright blood spread slowly outward from the motionless head. The thirsty earth soaked it up almost as fast as it seeped out from under the animal, leaving a dull beige patina on the irrregular stain in the earth.

It was a good horse and had served him well. Slocum turned his back and bent to pick up the saddlebags, then draped them over his shoulder. He loosened the bedroll and draped it over his other shoulder. Hoisting the heavy saddle, he rested it on the bedroll to cushion his shoulder from its weight. He was horseless and nearly broke. Montana seemed even bigger than before.

Slocum glanced at the sky, looking for the first sign of scavengers. The last thing he wanted to hear was the hungry screech of buzzards as they began to tear at the dead horse. The sky was still empty, not even a distant speck breaking the total blue waste.

He thanked his stars it was a cool morning. If heat had been added to the oppressive weight of his gear, he would have been finished. As it was, he had no idea how far he would have to walk. He stopped every half hour, to get a little water and to catch his breath. More than once, he thought about leaving the saddle behind, but he couldn't bear the thought. As it was, he had to buy a horse, which would cost several times what he had in his pockets. If he had to pick up a saddle, too, he might as well sell himself to the highest bidder. He'd be in hock for a year.

At the beginning of the third hour, he dropped the saddle and sat on it. The odd angle mocked him with its approximation of comfort. He opened one of the canteens and took a long pull. The water gurgled in the tin, more than half gone. He spat a thin paste of grit and water into the grass alongside the road, then took a second pull. He felt it trickle down his throat, not cold but at least palatable.

Slocum's legs and back ached. He debated making camp, but there seemed little point. Sooner or later he would have to carry his gear all the way to wherever it was he was going. Food was short and water getting shorter. He might get lucky, and he might not see anyone for a month.

He was about to get to his feet again when he spotted a small cloud of dust on the trail behind him. He decided to wait, and watched the cloud grow larger. He could hear the creak of the timbers long before he saw the wagon. When it finally appeared, it was just a blocky smudge, a little darker than the dust cloud.

A half hour later, the wagon creaked to a halt in front of him.

"Need a hand?"

The woman in the wagon smiled. There was no trace of mockery in it. Slocum nodded.

"Just throw that gear in the back. Mind you don't break anything."

Slocum tossed the saddle, saddlebags, and bedroll into the rear of the buckboard without bothering to lower the tailgate. He came around front and climbed into the passenger's seat. The young woman snapped the reins, and the horses moved off before she spoke again.

"I could sell you a horse, if you like. A good one."

"I could buy him, too. If I had the money."

"How much you got?"

"How much you selling the horse for?"

"Eighty dollars."

"Ain't got it." Slocum sighed.

"Well, I'll get you to town, anyway. Twin Trees. Maybe you can work something out there."

"I hope so."

"Where you headed?"

"Whitefish."

"That's a long way. Two hundred miles, maybe a little more."

"I know. Had a job waitin' there."

"You don't mind working, then." It wasn't a question, more a statement, as if it were an oddity worth remarking.

"No, ma'am, I don't. If the pay's fair and the work doable."

"What sort of work?"

"Not much I haven't done. Ranching, farming, you name it. Why?"

"I got some work. My name's Dawson, Lynn Dawson, by the way. Maybe we can work out a deal."

"I'm listening."

2

The wooden boards creaked like the joints of an old man. Slocum felt each squeal through the soles of his boots, feeling the sound rather than hearing it. He dropped to the ground, then sat on the low step, his heels scraping the dry earth in front of the house.

It was pitch black, except for the hard, sharp points of the stars, white against the dark sky. He'd just had his best meal in six months, and he didn't even have to pay for it. Lynn Dawson might be having a rough time of it as a rancher, but she sure as hell could cook.

Slocum reached into his vest for a cigarette. He'd rolled a few earlier, but hadn't smoked a single one. It was a habit he'd like to break, but there were times that seemed tailor-made for a smoke. This was one of them.

In the light from the ranch house, the barn and outbuildings looked white against the sky. The old wood, bleached by the sun, had taken on the look of old bone. The whole ghostly assemblage looked as if someone had constructed it from the ruins of a cemetery. He leaned back on his elbows, ignoring the blunt edge of the porch digging into his shoulder blades.

In the distance, he could hear the sounds of the night animals, edging closer and closer. When the lights were out, Slocum knew, they'd find their courage and prowl around the house and barn, drawn by the smell of the horses and cattle. The more ferocious might even claw at the house itself, attracted by the smell of sleep, the human scent slightly foul in the cold night air.

There was a screen door behind him, and Slocum could hear the scrape of a brush on the tin dishes, and the louder, clanging sound of the pots and pans banging against the galvanized tub. He sucked on the cigarette without really thinking about it, the smoke automatically entering his lungs and leaving them, as unconscious an action as breathing itself.

To Slocum's left, a bright block of orange light cut an angular path across the yard, tinting the dry soil. It looked almost like gold where it shaded back into the darkness. Slocum was bone-tired, and his shoulders ached from lugging the heavy saddle for a dozen miles. The bunkhouse, where he would sleep, was a stark gray-white hulk beyond the corral. A small lamp still burned, painting the windows pale yellow. He took a last unthinking drag on the cigarette, then tossed the stubby butt to the ground where he crushed it under his heel.

He got to his feet just as the screen door opened.

"I made some coffee," Lynn said. She elbowed her way through the door, letting it bang shut behind her. A heavy pewter mug in each hand, she walked carefully, stepping down to the ground and handing one of the mugs to Slocum. She turned her back to him and took a tentative sip of the hot coffee before sitting on the edge of the porch. She took care to keep one of the roof pillars between her and Slocum.

"Thanks," Slocum said, sipping from his own mug. "Good coffee, strong."

"Sam liked it that way. I guess I did too, after a while."

"Sam?"

"My husband . . ." She let it hang there, as if waiting for Slocum to ask.

He did. "What happened?"

Lynn took another sip of the coffee. Slocum glanced at her, afraid he might have upset her, but her face was impassive.

"An accident, I guess, I don't think I know for sure." She took another sip, then set the mug down on the rough boards of the porch. "He drank a little too much . . . a lot, actually. Doc Barstow kept telling him to take it easy, but Sam had a hard head. I don't know, maybe it wasn't an accident. Maybe he wanted it to happen. It was easier that way."

"Easier? Easier than what?"

"I don't know. What do people usually do when their lives are too much for them? Stick a gun in their mouths, cut their wrists? Sam was too subtle for that sort of thing. Besides, there was the insurance. It wasn't much, but it was like Sam to worry about that sort of thing. That's all he left for Amanda and me. That and the ranch. I guess I shouldn't complain. He *did* leave us that."

Slocum placed his own mug on the porch, then stood up. "Amanda's a good kid. You should be very proud of her."

"I am, I guess. But it's so hard to know what to do. Without a father, I think it's hard on her, hard in ways I can't imagine or understand."

"You were close to your own father?"

Lynn nodded. "Maybe that's why I'm so mad at Sam. I don't understand why he would do such a thing. Amanda should have mattered more to him than that."

"Maybe you're being too hard on him. Maybe it was an accident. You don't know that it wasn't."

"Not for sure, no. You're right. But . . ." She stopped when the hinges of the screen door squeaked again. Amanda Dawson stepped out onto the porch. Lynn glanced at her daughter, then turned quickly away, as if embarrassed to have been so open with a man she had just met.

"Good night, Mom. Night, Mr. Slocum."

"Good night, honey." Lynn watched Slocum as she spoke. He sensed her eyes on him but didn't look at her.

"Good night, Amanda."

The girl slipped back through the screen door, her bare feet slapping the floorboards. The kitchen lamp went out, and it suddenly got much darker in front of the house.

Lynn Dawson stood up, and Slocum watched her. She was a striking woman, her hair, a mass of thick, almost tangled curls, tumbled over her shoulders like dark water. Her face was almost perfect. Light bronze from the sun, a few freckles sprinkled under the color, testimony to her Irish roots, it seemed to have a life of its own. She laughed easily, and her mouth, its full lips a soft red even without lipstick, seemed almost sinful in its mobility. At dinner, Slocum had noticed her eyes, green like his own, but even deeper. They were shot through with gold highlights, the color of emeralds full of fire.

She was tall, maybe five six or seven, her height uncertain because of the boots. Slocum could only imagine her legs. They were long but not thin, a muscular strength noticeable through the second skin of bleached-out dungarees. But it was her chest that had fascinated him. Another handful of freckles danced in the open neck of her blue shirt, and the curve of full breasts tantalized him. Her body was so lush that simply breathing was an act of seduction.

"I guess I'll turn in too," she said. "Let me walk you to the bunkhouse."

"That's not necessary."

She ignored him and strode off toward the bunkhouse. Slocum hung back, watching her long legs, their tight muscularity supple under the tautness of faded denim. Her hips curved out sharply from a slender waist, then gently back toward her knees. The contours made a valentine of her ass. Slocum admired the view.

At the bunkhouse, Lynn stepped onto the full-length boardwalk, then leaned on one of the raw timbers supporting a split-shake ramada to keep off the sun and the rain. When Slocum joined her on the boardwalk, she stepped inside, nudging the half-open door aside with one hip.

He followed her in. The small lantern filled her hair with highlights. Slocum wondered just where his duties as an employee might take him.

"Got everything you need?" she asked.

"I think so, ma'am."

"It's Lynn, I told you."

"Lynn . . ."

She spun away from him, as if unable to look him in the eye. "If you think of anything you need . . ." She turned to him, her face not quite smiling, her lips moist from the darting tongue. "Just let me know."

He stepped toward her and leaned down. She tilted her head back a little, and his lips brushed hers. He reached for her just as she squirmed away, twisting her body to one side. His hand came to rest on one hip.

"I'm sorry," she whispered. "I shouldn't have done that. I just . . ."

"Never mind, Lynn. It's all right."

She nodded, still not facing him. "I'll see you in the morning," she whispered. She turned toward the door. From the side, he could see the tears on her cheeks, like small rivers of gold in the lantern light.

She ran out of the bunkhouse. Slocum walked to the window and watched her go. The house light went out almost immediately. He doused his own lantern and then pulled another cigarette from his vest pocket. Leaning on the windowsill, he lit the cigarette and let it dangle from his fingers. When it went out, unsmoked, he tossed it to the ground, then stripped for bed.

He lay there a long time, staring up at the dark ceiling. It was like a sky without stars. He tried to pierce it, as if to look beyond the wood and shingles, but the darkness remained impenetrable. Naked, his skin pebbled by the cool air drifting through the open window, he folded his arms behind his head, resigned to a night of uncertain sleep.

The first thud on the boardwalk was so soft, he wasn't sure he'd heard it. He half sat, straining his ears. The second thud was more definite. He looked toward the door, reaching for his Colt at the same time.

The screen door opened softly, as if someone were trying to suppress the noise of the hinges. A shadow stood in the doorway for a long moment, its hand on the door as if deciding whether or not to come in. Then the door closed softly and the shadow disappeared. Slocum walked to the door and stood in the opening.

"Lynn . . ." he called softly.

She stopped and turned slowly back to him. He could barely see in the moonless dark.

Tentatively, she stepped back toward the bunkhouse. He could see now that her feet and legs were bare. The work shirt hung loosely. She stepped onto the boardwalk, her feet silent on the hard wood. Her movements were slow, almost dreamlike. He thought of a girl he had known years before, a tomboy who loved to skinny-dip in a small pond. He remembered the way her body, so different from his, looked under water, the ways its curves seemed designed for the water, so fluid, so sleek.

Then Lynn Dawson opened the door. She realized for the first time that he was naked. He thought she smiled. With a soft hiss, the shirt fell to the floor and she was naked as he was. She stepped toward him and the screen door thumped against its frame. She took another step. He could smell the cologne, just a hint in the cool air.

He leaned forward, reaching for her, but she was quicker. Her hand found his cock, already stiff, and she moaned. Her fingers slipped along its length, as if exploring something they had never felt before.

His hands were on her shoulders. Her skin was so smooth and cold, it felt like silk under a thin sheet of ice. She began to stroke him, the tight fist squeezing him just hard enough. Slowly, her hand unhampered by the awkward angle, she brought him to a hardness so perfect he thought he might be turning to stone. Falling away from his hands, she sank to her knees.

He felt the soft tangle of her hair brush against his thighs, then the heat of her tongue snaking along his length, leaving a scalding slickness. The tongue darted this way and that, then, like a live thing, curled around the head of his cock. He felt her lips open slightly, her tongue withdrawing to accommodate him.

Her sharp, even teeth teased him, nipping and tugging, grabbing the flesh of him just behind the head. Her tongue twirled and she darted her head forward, suddenly taking in as much of him as she could. As he groaned, she snapped back to leave him dangling. In the cool breeze through the door, her saliva felt cold.

She stood up and pressed herself against him, standing on tiptoe and opening her legs just enough to allow his cock to slide between them. He felt another, warmer fluid. The crisp hair of her bush mingled with his own as she wrapped her arms around him. Her breasts pressed against his chest, their nipples hard against his cold skin.

She worked her hips back and forth, squeezing his cock with her thighs. Slowly, like a practiced partner, she brought him still higher, never quite letting him slip away. Slocum felt her juices beginning to slide down his thighs and he grabbed her ass to hold her to him.

"Not yet," she whispered. "Not yet. I'm . . ."

Slocum lifted her off her feet and backed toward the bunk. He felt it with the backs of his knees and tilted over, pulling Lynn down on top of him. She scrambled, and he thought for a minute she was going to leave. Instead, she straddled him, grabbing his cock with one hand and stroking it again. He strained upward, and she obliged, shifting her hips and then suddenly letting herself go. He slid in all the way, and she moaned. He strained upward again, this time lifting her weight with his thrust. She bent forward, pressing him back onto the mattress. "Let me," she whispered.

Straightening, she grabbed his hands and brought them to her breasts, folding his fingers around their fullness. He massaged the nipples with slow fingers as Lynn began to rise and fall. Slowly her tempo increased, each time rising until he nearly slipped out, then tantalizingly reimpaling herself.

Slocum let his hands slide along the curves of her ribs, coming to rest on her broad hips. He held her, gently guiding her to alter her rhythm. Faster and faster, her mouth open, panting, she rose and fell. With each fall she twisted her hips first left, then right, then left again, as if she wanted to screw him into herself permanently. Slocum moved his own hips in time to hers, and when her moan rose to a scream, he felt himself let go, the tightness in him exploding with spurt after spurt, as if he were emptying himself into her.

She went limp, throwing her head back so far he felt her hair brush his knees. He ran his callused hands up along her ribs, the fingers tracing rivulets of sweat until they found her breasts. He cupped them and squeezed gently. She moaned again and he let them go.

Sliding back to her hips, he slowly lifted her, backing away as he did. Then, pulling her down, he pressed upward, trying to pierce into the very center of her weight. She responded almost at once, and this time she let him set the pace. He could feel the sweat dripping from her body, smell the salty tang of her juices, and the scent of her spurred him on.

This time she didn't scream, just letting a long, slow moan escape around her tongue, squeezed between half-clenched teeth. Suddenly she slipped off him. He thought she was going to lie beside him.

The screen door banged softly and she was gone.

3

The sun was hotter than Slocum had anticipated. It pounded down on him like an invisible, unrelenting hammer. Its pulsing rhythm echoed in his head. He could feel the blood throbbing in his temples as he wielded the heavy sledge. It was only ten-thirty, and already he felt as if he had been working all day.

He tossed the hammer to the turf and trudged back to the wagon. Most of the posts he had loaded that morning still lay in the bottom of the buckboard, their sharpened ends poking out over the open tailgate, threatening him like the teeth of a wild animal. He hauled another of the heavy posts from the wagon and hoisted it to his shoulder. Staggering in the uneven grass, he found the next hole, tipped the stake into it, point down, and held it upright while he kicked dirt back into the hole.

When enough dirt had been replaced to keep the post upright, he bent to pick up the heavy sledge. Curling it far behind him, he brought it up and over in a perfect arc. He grunted each time the blunt end of the hammer struck the top of the post. The shock ran down his arms, rattled his shoulders in their sockets, then raced down his spine. He traced the ragged line of posts with his eye. Nearly two dozen had been driven home, but more than three times that many remained to be seated.

Slocum slammed the sledge into the post once more,

just to make certain, then tossed the heavy hammer aside. He kicked the rest of the dirt into the hole. The balance of the damp earth he packed around the post in a steep cone, stamping it tight with the sole of his boot. When he was finished, he tried the post, shaking it with his right hand. It felt firm, barely wiggling in the tightly packed soil. He tamped the dirt one more time, then walked back to the wagon.

Slocum climbed up into the seat, uncoiled the reins and kicked off the brake. He nudged the horse forward another thirty yards, then braked. He locked the wagon down, re-coiled the reins around the brake handle, and jumped down. Reaching under the seat, he tugged a canteen free and shook it. The water sloshing around inside sounded better than it tasted. He opened the canteen, took a long pull on the water and screwed the lid back into place.

John Slocum was not unused to hard work, but this was more than he had bargained for. Lynn Dawson better have a damned good horse for him when this was all over. He grinned at the thought, then dropped to the grass to get out of the sun for a few minutes.

The gap in the fence was nearly a quarter mile long. Lynn didn't know whether it had always been there, or if someone had dismantled some of Sam's handiwork. Slocum had prowled around, but aside from a few scuffed patches of grass, there was no indication that the fence had ever been joined. Maybe Sam had gotten tired of it. Maybe he had died before getting a chance to finish it. Hell, any-thing was possible. Maybe somebody had been paid to do it and had cheated Sam out of some of the money. What-ever the reason, the gap was there. And until it no longer was, Slocum would be able to think about nothing else. It was his first assignment, and it was a bastard of a job.

He'd run fence before, but never alone. He glanced at his hands, easing them into the sunlight to see them more clearly. Callused palms and fingers were beginning to glow a soft red. Before long, he knew, a few blisters, taking advantage of the few tender spots left him, would make handling the hammer a painful chore.

The gap was nearly five hundred yards wide. Spacing the posts every five yards was the best he could hope for. Any more and the wire would sag; any less and he'd never finish. Even so, it didn't take anything more complicated than long division to figure out he'd be planting a hundred posts. He had to dig a hundred holes to do it. The turf was tough, and the soil beneath it tougher still. Even with the post-hole digger, it was rough going.

He started to wonder whether Lynn Dawson was taking advantage of him. His shoulders said yes, but when he thought of the previous night, he couldn't believe it. He was getting as good as he gave. Truth to tell, he might be slightly ahead of the bargain. If there was a repeat performance, he'd be a clear winner.

It was time to get back to work, and Slocum climbed reluctantly to his feet. As he walked back to the fence line, he stared across the open range. Far in the distance he caught a slight movement of dark brown. He squinted against the sun's glare, trying to resolve the blurred image to something comprehensible. It appeared to be a handful of cattle, but they were too far away for him to be sure. It could be a small group of pronghorns, or maybe some wild horses. For a moment he thought it might be the latter, and it dawned on him that if he could capture an appropriate mount he could call off his bargain with Lynn Dawson.

Then he remembered the look on her face this morning, and the reason for it, and he wondered whether any man was strong enough to walk away from a bargain like his. On the other hand, he still had the possibility of that job in Whitefish, although he knew the chances for it were fading quickly. He was still four days' ride away, and it might take him that long before the horse was broken and sufficiently reliable to attempt so long a ride.

Slocum wished he had binoculars. He screwed his eyes shut even tighter and still was unable to decide what he was watching. He knew Lynn had lost quite a few head of cattle in the past year, and there was a chance that this might be some of her livestock. He walked back to the wagon and unhitched the small mare tethered to the rear.

Slocum swung into the saddle, deciding even as he did so that he had nothing to lose by checking it out. Besides, he told himself, his shoulders hurt and he could use an hour's rest. He kicked the little mare into a gallop and plunged through the fence break. The ground sloped gently down to a broad valley, then climbed just as gently upward, peaking higher on the far side. Whatever it was he had seen, it was still there, but hidden now by a stand of box elders.

Despite its small size, the horse was graceful and powerful. She raced easily over the grassy turf, kicking aside late fall wildflowers sprinkled in the knee-high grass. The mare seemed to sense unevenness in the ground beneath her, moving from side to side to skirt the rougher terrain.

Slocum could still see the dark smudge, beyond the trees now and moving up-country. In a few minutes they would crest the next ridge and disappear from sight. If he lost them, he wasn't sure he could find them again. This was far from familiar territory, and he wasn't sure how much he wanted to get involved with Lynn Dawson's affairs. Doing a job of work was one thing; investing part of himself, however small, in her affairs was something else again. And that something was about as treacherous as a quagmire. Once in, he might never get out. And settling down was the farthest thing from his mind.

He had to admit that if he were interested he could do worse than Lynn Dawson—a hell of a lot worse. But that was a mighty big "if" to have to deal with on such short acquaintance. He knew it was a bad sign that he was already thinking in such terms, but that was a testimony to Lynn and her charms. He couldn't begrudge her that, but he didn't have to fall over like a lovesick pup and lick her boots, either.

Not that she had asked him to.

Hell, he thought, all I'm doing is running some fence and checking on some strays. That doesn't mean I have to marry the damned woman. And he smiled, knowing that his presumption might surprise her. They had had a tumble. Both of them had enjoyed it, that was abundantly clear. But whether Lynn Dawson thought it was anything more than that was something Slocum wouldn't want to stake his life on guessing.

He hit the broad bottom of the valley and began to pick up his pace. The mare was running easily under him, barely raising a sweat on the gentle slope. High above him, near the top of the green ridge, he could see a small cluster of animals. Now that he was closer, it was obvious they were cattle. Whether they carried the Lazy D brand of the Dawson ranch was another matter, however.

The knee-deep grasses began to thin, giving way to a sparser, tougher growth, and the mare slowed her pace a bit. Slocum still had half a mile to go when he heard the first report. It echoed from a distance, and under the broad sky it was difficult to place. He cocked an ear, hoping for a repeat. The second shot came a few seconds later, and one of the steers stumbled and fell. Somebody was shooting at them. A third shot kicked up a puff of dust to the left of the small knot of cows. This time, Slocum was able to place the location of the shooter.

Standing in the stirrups to get a better look, he spotted a small patch of canvas in a clump of trees near the ridge. It looked like a wagon cover, but he couldn't be sure. Kicking the mare in the flanks, he goosed her into a fast gallop and rapidly narrowed the gap.

As he reached the fringes of some tangled brush, a fourth shot rang out. This one, too, missed. Whoever it was with the rifle was a lousy shot. That was just as well. Slocum skidded to a halt and leapt off the mare, leaving her to stand idly, trailing the reins in the grass. He walked quickly to the downed steer and knelt beside it.

The animal had been struck in the front leg, the bullet breaking bone and ripping through the thick muscle just above the ankle. The steer was struggling to rise, but the leg couldn't support its weight. He patted the animal on the muzzle, then moved toward its hindquarters, where he spotted the distinctive "D" lying on its side, burned high on the left flank.

It was Lynn Dawson's steer, all right, but it was as good as dead. He'd have to butcher the carcass on the spot and haul the meat back in the wagon.

Slocum stood up and looked toward the stand of small trees. From this angle, he could clearly see the outline of three wagons. All of them had seen better days. The shooting had stopped, and he wondered whether he had scared them into passivity or if they had their sights on other game. The clearing seemed deserted, but he drew his Colt Navy, holding it at his thigh as he approached.

At fifty yards, Slocum called a loud hello and waited for a response. The greeting was ignored, and Slocum walked closer. When he reached the wagons he wondered where everyone was. He called hello again, and this time someone shouted back from the third wagon. Slocum approached it carefully, pushing the canvas flap aside to peer into the darkness.

"Howdy, friend," someone said. From the slurred speech, Slocum guessed the man was drunk. "You're just in time for a cookout."

"I don't imagine you mean that seriously," Slocum said. "At least, I hope not."

"Hell yes, man. Ain't had steak in weeks, none of us. 'Bout time we stoked up on some real good chuck."

"That steer doesn't belong to you."

Instead of answering, the man jumped down from the wagon. He seemed to be biding his time for something, and Slocum was getting edgy. With three wagons, there had to be at least two other men, and he hadn't seen another soul.

The man staggered a bit, catching himself up on the end of the wagon and holding on to keep himself upright. "That your cow, friend?"

"No."

"Then what are you bellyachin' about?"

"It belongs to the woman I work for."

The man laughed, splattering saliva in all directions. "Keerist, friend, you take orders from a skirt? What kind of man are you?"

"An honest one. Which is more than I can say for you. Where'd your friends go?"

"Whatsamatter? Nervous? Hell, I don't need no help to wipe the ass of some clown who works for a woman. I might not even bother. No gain. It'd be like kickin' a dead horse."

Slocum heard hoofbeats and turned to look back down the slope. Seven or eight mounted men were galloping toward the wagons. Slocum eased to the left, keeping one eye on the drunk and the other on the approaching men. "You're going to have to pay for that steer," he said.

"Hell, they was wild stock. Don't belong to nobody."

"You check the brand?"

"Didn't have none."

"You check?"

"Didn't have to. I know."

"You don't know shit," Slocum said.

The rest of the men reached the wagons, and their horses kicked up knots of grass and clumps of dirt, scattering dust on Slocum and the drunk alike.

The apparent leader of the group, a big, bearded man in a duster, jumped from his horse. "What's the trouble here?" he demanded. He was staring at the drunk, but the question clearly was addressed to Slocum.

"Your friend here killed a cow that don't belong to him. I think maybe he ought to pay up, and maybe sober up while he's at it."

"Damnit, Jed," the big man said, "I told you I didn't want no trouble." He turned to Slocum. "Seems like to me maybe you don't deserve no payment. I don't see no fences, and I don't see no sign. Them there cattle could belong to anybody."

"They could, but they don't."

"That's right, Clyde," the drunk laughed, "they belong to some woman. Big shot here takes his orders from a skirt. I ought not to pay him just on account of that. But I will, though."

The drunk staggered toward Slocum, who circled a bit to keep all the men in sight. The drunk was reaching for his back pocket as he stood wavering in front of Slocum. His breath stank of cheap whiskey. Suddenly he leaned forward and planted a wet kiss on Slocum's cheek. "There, you give that to your lady boss with my compliments. Tell her I'd like to give it to her personal, but I wouldn't want to catch the crabs. You can do that for me, sonny boy." Jed had a friendly audience and he knew it. They didn't disappoint them.

Slocum was not amused. He swung his free hand, his fist catching the drunken Jed on the point of the chin. The man staggered back and landed on his butt, then fell over on his side. Cocking the colt, Slocum eyeballed the big

man while he bent down and fished Jed's wallet out of his
pocket.

Straightening up, he pulled a sheaf of crumpled bills
from the wallet and tossed the ragged leather to the ground.
He sorted through the bills, found a pair that seemed like a
fair price, and rained the others over Jed's stomach.

"Now, unless you got some good reason to hang around
here," Slocum said, "and I don't believe you do, not one
that would convince me anyway, I suggest you boys move
on. Pronto."

"Now hold on a minute, cowboy." Clyde took a step
forward. "You got no call to be givin' me orders. Clyde
Lavalle is his own boss. 'Sides, this ain't your land, nor
your lady friend's neither."

"Maybe not. But I'll tell you what. You're here tomor-
row morning, when I come back, you'll wish you took my
advice."

Lavalle, conscious of his men waiting for him to make a
move, stepped closer to Slocum. One of the others, sidling
in behind the big man, was out of Slocum's sight. Lavalle
moved a step closer, then darted to one side.

The shot took all three men by surprise.

The man behind Lavalle, as slender as the skinning
knife that dropped from his hand, gripped his wrist. Blood
oozed between his fingers, staining the bright blade before
slipping off into the grass.

Lynn Dawson smiled at Slocum as she levered another
round into the carbine's chamber. The bright arc of the
ejected shell seemed to linger in the air long after the
empty round disappeared in the grass.

"I think you heard Mr. Slocum, boys. I'd move on, I
was you."

4

Slocum climbed into the saddle without looking at Lynn Dawson. He watched the whiskey runners hustle their wagons out of the trees and head over the top of the ridge. Several of the men turned in their saddles and stared back at Slocum as they began the long downhill run to the bottom of the next valley. Far below, a narrow band of water reflected the brilliant sun. It looked like liquid fire as the sunlight splashed around the rocks, glancing off in every direction.

Lynn poked him with a sharp finger. "Anything wrong, John?"

"I hope not. But I don't know."

"What do you mean? You're not worried about those men, are you?"

"Worried? No, but something tells me we haven't seen the last of them."

"We? I like the sound of that."

"You know what I mean," Slocum snapped at her, and was almost immediately sorry. "I mean . . . Ah, the hell with it."

"No, tell me what you meant."

"All I meant was, they don't strike me as the type to forgive and forget."

"Forgive? What in hell do they *have* to forgive. It was my steer they slaughtered."

"You think it matters to them? You think they give a good goddamn about the law, and ownership. They live by one rule—if you want something, you take it."

"I think you're overreacting."

"I hope I am." Slocum wheeled the mare and started toward the dead steer. "I think I better butcher that animal. It won't do to let the blood set in him too long. The meat will spoil."

"What's the difference, there's no way we can use it all before it spoils anyway."

"We can smoke it. It'll keep."

"I don't know how to do that."

"Never mind, I'll take care of it. Why don't you go get the wagon?"

Lynn nodded and moved off without looking back. She seemed offended by something, but Slocum had long since given up trying to figure out what pissed women off. It was easier to wait and apologize when they were ready to forgive. And if they never got around to it . . . well, there would always be another.

Slocum watched her go for a few seconds, then took a lariat and looped it over the steer's head. He dragged the animal to the tallest of the trees in the small stand, then dismounted. He took the rope off and used a rawhide thong to lash the animals rear legs together. Slipping a tight loop around the steer's bound legs, he snugged the knot as tightly as he could, then climbed back into the saddle, trailing the lariat from his left hand.

Tossing the rope over a sizable limb, he grabbed the free end and looped it around the saddle horn. Urging the mare to back up, he watched the carcass slowly rise into the air, hindquarters first. When the dead steer's rear hooves scraped against the limb, its head dangled a scant few inches off the ground. It wasn't as high as he'd like, but it would have to do.

Dismounting, he picked up the skinning knife that still lay where it had fallen. He tested the edge with his thumb and, satisfied, drew it quickly across the steer's throat. The blood oozed out, and Slocum opened the throat wider. It was best to let an animal's beating heart purge its veins, but gravity would have to suffice this time.

Slocum stood close to the steer's belly, careful to avoid the pool of thickening blood gathering under the gaping throat. Deftly, he eviscerated the steer. The steaming innards accumulated in a pile to his left. He'd never butchered a steer before, but he'd dressed deer killed on hunting trips with his old man, and more than a few hogs had gone to the smokehouse after his surgical ministrations. It wasn't all that different, just bigger.

When the visceral cavity was clean, he stood back to check his handiwork, then bent to wipe his bloody hands on the saw-edged grass. Even in the cool air, flies had begun to gather. Their buzzing sounded like a distant sawmill. He wiped his boots on the grass, then walked out into the open to watch the receding wagons jouncing across the bottom of the valley.

Slocum wanted to believe Lynn was right, but in his heart he knew she couldn't have been more wrong. Lavalle was not the type to take a loss so easily. And it was evident, although Lynn seemed not to have understood, that Lavalle and his men were running whiskey, most probably to the Indians. Jed's mistake had not been in shooting the steer, although that, too, was an error in judgment. His real failure was in hitting the goods while the rest of the runners were off doing whatever it was they had been doing. And that, too, was of concern to Slocum.

It didn't strike him as likely that they had been in town for morning church services. It wouldn't have been for supplies, because they would have taken at least one of the wagons. That left the question open. What in hell *were* they up to? Slocum had no idea, but whatever it might be, he was sure he wouldn't like it. The last thing Montana needed was more trouble with the Indians.

Crook and his bullies in blue had been worrying Sioux and Comanche, Blackfoot and Cheyenne from one end of the plains to the other. The Indians themselves were not kindly disposed to white men in recent years, whether they were in uniform or not. For the most part, they just wanted to be left alone. But whiskey did funny things. It wasn't that the Indians were any worse than white men, just that they were easier victims of the demon rum. Unused to it, having nothing nearly so strong in their own culture, they fell prey to its baser effects before they even realized something had gone wrong. Mix the whiskey and the ill feelings together and you had a cocktail only a devil could love.

And while Slocum was wondering about Lavalle and his men, he himself was not being neglected by their considerations. Lavalle had taken the reins of one of the wagons, forcing Jed to sit beside him. He had driven for half an hour without a word, but when the wagon hit bottom and he turned to the west, using the sandy bank of the Sweetgum as a highway, he jabbed Jed with a pointed elbow.

"I told you once, I told you a thousand times, Jed, stay the hell out of the goods. That whiskey's for sellin', not for drinkin'."

"Damn, Clyde. A man gets thirsty out here. Hell, I might as well be in the middle of the damn desert, I can't have a taste once in a while."

"You have another taste without me sayin' so, Jed, and you'll wish to hell you *were* in the goddamn desert. I swear, I'll skin you alive, you tap another keg."

"I don't see what the big deal is."

"I already told you, Indians don't want to buy no open keg. Ever' one you tap is one I can't sell, except to some hard-up barkeep. Thing is, he knows what it's worth. The

Indian don't. I can make three, four times the money. I wanted to sell to white men, I'd find me another line of work, sellin' something makes a real profit."

"You say so, I guess it has to be that way. But I don't like it much."

"You don't have to like it, Jed. You just have to do like I say. I pay your wages, and you're already into me for three kegs. I ought to dock you the price I charge redskins, but I'm lettin' you off easy. But, I swear to God, you do it again, you got two choices."

"Which are?"

"You can pay me the Indian price. For all four. Or you can have a bullet in the damn head. You pick it."

"All right, all right. I get the point."

"You damn well better keep gettin' it, Jed, 'cause I ain't jokin' no more. It costs too much."

Lavalle was about to continue in the same vein when one of his men pulled alongside the wagon. "We got to talk, Clyde, soon's you get a minute."

Lavalle looked at the man, his face screwed into a puzzle. "What's the matter?"

"Nothing. I just want to talk a bit."

Lavalle stuck his hand out as a signal to the other wagons, then braked his own, allowing the heavy schooner to roll to a shuddering halt. He stood up in the seat and leaned past the canvas cover. "Chow," he bellowed, then jumped down from the wagon.

Jed followed him to the ground, intrigued by the urgency in the other man's voice. While Lavalle bellowed instructions to the others, Jed sidled alongside the rider. "What is it, Ralphie."

"Ain't nothing that concerns you, Jed."

"Hell, I work for Lavalle too, don't I?"

"Not so far as I can tell, you don't, no. I ain't seen you work a lick since you hired on."

Jed scowled at the taller man. "Ralphie, you makin' me mad, you talkin' like that."

"Well, I'll tell you what, Jed. Why don't you just make me shut up? How about that? You think you can do that?" Ralphie balled his fist and waved the left one under Jed's nose.

Jed brushed the hand away, laughing. "Come on, now, Ralphie, why don't you ease up, huh? It don't matter none." He turned away, took a small step, then swung back around, bringing his left up in a tight arc. The punch caught the larger man by surprise, striking him in the gut and knocking the wind from his lungs.

Ralphie went to his knees, clutching his stomach. He dry-heaved once, then threw up all over Jed's shoes. "You sonofabitch," he mumbled, spitting in an effort to rid his mouth of the bilious taste. "I ought to kill you for that."

"Think you can do that, Ralphie, huh? Think you can?"

Ralphie climbed to his feet, one hand massaging his bruised stomach muscles. He was about to charge headlong at his assailant when he heard Lavalle's voice calling him away from Jed.

"What the hell is going on here? Ralphie, what happened?"

"I'll tell you what happened. This drunken sumbitch sucker punched me, that's what happened."

"Hell's bells, Ralphie, you let a broken-down alky like Jed sucker-punch you, you got no right to complain. You ought to be ashamed of yourself."

"Fuck that. I don't know why you let that bastard hang around."

"Oh, now, Jed has his uses. See, the thing about him, he's willing to do stuff. Stuff other men might be too . . . squeamish to do. That makes him pretty valuable. Specially in this line of work. Hell, Ralphie, I got close to two hundred kegs in them wagons. I play my cards right, I can get near a hundred dollars worth of skins a keg. But it takes doin', and it sometimes takes doin' stuff you and me wouldn't be proud of ourselves if we done 'em. Jed ain't like that. He's got no pride. That makes him useful. You might even say valuable."

"Maybe so, if you say so."

"I do say so. Now, what do you want to tell me?"

Ralphie walked away, waving Lavalle to follow him. When he had some distance between himself and the wagons, he waved Lavalle closer.

"What you acting so mysterious about, Ralphie?"

"I don't know, maybe nothing. Maybe not."

"Spit it out, goddamn it. I ain't got all day."

"That guy..."

"What guy?"

"That guy back there, where Jed killed the steer."

"What about him?"

"He look familiar to you?"

"No. Should he?"

"I dunno. I think I seen him before. Not him, I mean, but a picture."

"So what, so you seen his picture. What's all the mystery?"

"I think I seen him on a wanted poster. In fact, I'm sure I did."

"So what?"

"There's a reward for 'im. A big one."

"Hell, so what. There's a price on my head, too." Lavalle waved disgustedly. "You called me over here for this garbage?"

"Five hundred dollars sound like garbage to you, Clyde? It sure don't to me."

"Five hundred? You sure?"

"I ain't got the poster on me, but, yeah, I'm sure. And I

was thinkin', you know, we could grab him, turn him in at Butte. Collect the reward."

"I don't think I'd get more than a passing glance from any marshal. I'd be lucky he didn't throw me in jail myself."

"Maybe so, but I still got friends. Six years a marshal earns you a little somethin'. That's where I seen his picture. It's a federal rap. I could turn him in to Jerry Hollingsworth, in Butte. Jerry owes me one."

Lavalle stroked his beard absently. He seemed on the verge of turning away. Ralphie pushed him. "What do you think, Clyde, it's worth a shot, ain't it?"

"Suppose he's the wrong guy?"

"What's he going to do, sue us?"

Lavalle liked that. He laughed, then slapped Ralphie on the back. "I guess you're right. But we got to do this right. How do you figure we get our hands on him? He seems like a tough man to hog-tie."

"Well, I been thinkin' about that. I don't know if I want to do it, but it might work. Probably would."

"'Probably' won't get it done, Ralphie. We got to have something surefire. I don't want to mess this up. Somebody could get dead in a hurry messin' with that fellow."

"Didn't you say Jed had his uses?"

Lavalle laughed. "Now that you mention it, I believe I did say that, didn't I? Well, what do you know?"

"Here's what I figure," Ralphie said, tugging Lavalle a little farther away from the wagons.

Lavalle listened carefully. When Ralphie was done, Lavalle went back to pulling his beard. He was silent for a long time. "What the hell?" he finally said. "What have we got to lose?"

5

Bob Kennedy dropped the heavy sack of beans onto the counter. With a stubby pencil from behind his ear, he drew a thick black line on a sheet of paper curling at both ends. Replacing the pencil, he shifted his glasses and walked the length of the counter, hefting a wooden ladder against his prominent middle. He set the ladder down in the far corner, hitched up his apron, then started the climb.

Near the top rung, he turned to look over his shoulder. "You sure you need this much rice, Amanda?"

"Twenty pounds, that's what Mom told me to get."

"Seems like you folks must be part Chinese, you need all this rice all of a sudden. Lynn, your momma, used to only get ten pounds, and not too often at that."

"That was when we were alone. We got some help now. We need more, I guess, on account of Mr. Slocum."

"Slocum, Slocum. Humh, don't think I know him. Local fella, is he?" Kennedy stopped reaching for the sack of rice to peer at Amanda over the tops of his glasses. He nearly lost his balance, and grabbed onto the top shelf just as the ladder started to slip out from under him.

"You all right, Mr. Kennedy?"

"Oh, don't worry about me, Amanda, I've fallen off better ladders than this. You get used to it after a while. I remember once I had two fifty-pound sacks of flour, one on each shoulder, and I fell right over the counter with 'em. That hurt for a while. Didn't bust the sacks, though. Folks talked about that for a couple years. Thought I was some kind of magician."

"Well, I'd just as soon you don't repeat that, not for my sake." Amanda laughed, and Kennedy stared at her for a moment, as if puzzled. Then, when it dawned on him what she meant, he grinned.

"Don't worry, Mandy. I'm too old for that sort of shenanigan these days." He hefted the sack onto his shoulder then climbed down slowly, one hand holding the sack in place, the other holding on to the splintery wooden rail of the old ladder.

He dumped the sack with a hissing thud on the counter. "Where'd you say this Slocum fella comes from?" He checked the list, crossing off the rice while he waited for an answer.

"I didn't say, actually. Fact is, I don't know. I don't know if Mom knows, either."

Kennedy frowned. "Not a good idea, you know, lettin' strangers get too close. Especially two women alone. And a fine-looking woman like your momma, well . . . you know how men are. Or maybe you don't. Leastways, I hope you don't. I guess I shouldn't even be saying anything. None of my business. But you tell your ma to be careful, you hear? Tell her Bob Kennedy worries about her."

"I'm sure we'll be fine, Mr. Kennedy. Mr. Slocum seems a perfect gentleman."

"Sleeps in the bunkhouse, does he?"

Amanda glared at him. "Where else *would* he sleep?"

"You're right, Mandy. It's none of my business. Still, you ladies be careful."

Kennedy, a flush of pink peeking out from around his

starched white collar, turned to the list again. He was anxious to get his foot out of his mouth. Moving up and down the aisle behind the counter like a new curator at a museum, taking stock of his collection, the portly shopkeeper assembled the rest of Amanda Dawson's order.

When the supplies formed a mound on the countertop, Kennedy called his stock boy from the back room. Together the two men lugged the heavy sacks to the wagon tied up out front. Amanda settled her mother's account and climbed into the wagon seat while the last packages were loaded.

Kennedy closed the tailgate, slipped the locking pins into place, and walked to the driver's side of the wagon. He uncoiled the reins and held them for a moment. "You and your mom be careful, Mandy," he said.

Mandy looked at him without saying anything. Kennedy seemed on the verge of apologizing again, but he thought better of it. Amanda snapped the reins, and the team threw its shoulders into the traces. The wagon jerked once, then started to roll, its wheels creaking under the load. A moment later the horses hit their stride. Kennedy stood on the wooden sidewalk and watched her. The stock boy stood to his left.

When Kennedy noticed him, he said, "Never you mind, Petey. You got a few years yet before you get involved with that sort of thing. So does Mandy, God willing. Life's complicated enough."

Petey didn't answer. He stood there, hands on hips, long after Amanda was little more than a flag of dark hair waving over a wagonload of groceries.

Kennedy had to come back out of the store and call him inside. "Pretty thing, she is, Petey. But that's a trap, mind what I'm tellin' you. The prettier they are, the bigger fools they make of us."

"She's welcome to make a fool of me anytime, Mr. Kennedy."

"Then it's a certain thing she will."

Slocum finished planting the last post and tossed the hammer to the ground with a grunt of satisfaction. He clapped his sore hands together, then examined the blistered palms. It had been a long time since he'd last pushed himself so much. He was starting to wonder why he was working so hard. Every blow of the sledge had felt good to him. He derived a certain proprietary pleasure in watching the row of poles narrow the gap. It couldn't have felt much better if the spread had been his own. He knew the feeling, and it scared him.

It would be so easy to let himself get trapped by Lynn Dawson. Not that she was in any way trying to trap him. But maybe that's why it would be so easy. She was the most easygoing woman he'd ever met. Her manner was as natural as an old friend. And her beauty was not even a factor in the equation. It was as if she didn't even realize how attractive she was, which served only to make her more appealing still.

Slocum flopped down in the shade and lay flat on his back. The weight on his shoulders and the ache in his spine seemed to drain away. It was time for lunch, but he didn't feel hungry. It was too pretty a day to worry about something so ordinary as food. The cool air snapped around him like an invisible whip. It flowed like cool water across his skin, and he closed his eyes for a moment, letting the after-image of the sun fade away against the thin sheet of blood in his lids.

Idly, he dug his hands into the tall grass, feeling the rasp of the blade edges as he let them slide between his fingers. The smell of the rich soil—a dark, musty scent—filled his nostrils, and he wriggled his shoulders to flatten himself still more, to get closer to the earth.

High above him he heard the cry of a hawk, and he opened his eyes to slits. He spotted the bird almost immediately, a black blade slicing through the blue air like a knife. It dropped suddenly earthward, but Slocum didn't want to look. He knew that the bird's descent could end in one of two ways—either the frustration of failure, or the bloody triumph of a successful hunt. He was in the mood neither for disappointment, even that of the bird, or the gory reality that was nature. It was nice, on this beautiful day, to be a little ignorant, to dream a little, and to pretend that the world as it was was closer to perfect than he knew it to be.

Slocum inhaled deeply, then let the air out of his lungs in a long, slow hiss, the way he'd done as a child on those few days cold enough to make a cloud of his breath. It was a rare enough thing in Georgia that it seemed just a little mysterious, even a bit sinister. Those were days when magic was a good thing. It was pleasant to deceive himself a little, as if that magic were still possible.

And he knew it was Lynn Dawson who did it to him, who made him just a bit foolish in his own eyes, and just courageous enough not to care. He could feel her skin under his fingers, the weight of her breasts in his hands, and it made him want her with him. He imagined the weight of her, pressing him to the ground, and thought maybe that was the only way he could manage to be as close to the earth as he wanted to be at that moment.

His eyes still closed, he began to drift off, and the pounding of his own blood in his ears took on the ominous insistence of thunder. It took him several seconds to realize the thunder was approaching hooves. He jerked upright, stood, and reached for his gunbelt, coiled in the wagon bed.

Jumping to his feet, he pulled the Colt from his holster and peered around the wagon. Convinced that Lavalle and his cronies had returned, he cocked the pistol and waited for the approaching rider to come up over the ridge line. He zeroed in on the source of the hoofbeats and held his breath.

The horse's head broke the horizon first. He recognized the distinctive diamond blaze at once. Uncocking the Colt, he slipped it back into the holster and reached for his shirt as Lynn Dawson skidded to a halt. Scrambling into the sleeves, he got tangled up, and felt just a little silly as she jumped down.

"Don't dress on my account," she said. "God knows..."

"What are you doing here?" Slocum continued to struggle with the sleeves, finally getting both arms through. He tucked the tails in without buttoning it.

"I got tired of waiting for Mandy and the supplies. I thought maybe you could use some lunch." Lynn yanked saddlebags from the back of her horse and walked toward the wagon. Dropping to one knee, she opened one of the bags and jerked a gingham tablecloth free of the leather. The other bag surrendered sandwiches and fruit, along with a small bottle of red wine.

Lynn looked up at him and smiled. "Anyone for a picnic?"

Without waiting for an answer, she spread the cloth in the shadow cast by the wagon and unwrapped the food. Returning to the saddlebags, she took two tin cups. "I'd have brought the good crystal, but I didn't think it would have survived the trip. Besides, I broke it all the last time Sam and I had a fight."

Slocum felt his jaw drop, but he said nothing.

"Don't gape," Lynn said. "Sit down. Eat."

Like a child hopelessly bewildered by adult instructions, Slocum looked at the food, then at Lynn, then back at the food spread out on the tablecloth.

Without waiting for him, Lynn started to eat. She took a few mouthfuls of food, then popped the pre-loosened cork on the wine and poured a little in both cups. "If you don't hurry up, there won't be time for anything else."

"Else? What else?"

"Never mind."

Slocum sat on the corner of the cloth and took the wine she offered. He sipped it and made a face.

"I'm not surprised. I didn't figure you for a wine man."

"What kind of man do you figure me to be?" Slocum asked.

"I don't. Not yet. But I'm working on it."

She ran a finger from his throat to his beltline, scraping the skin of his chest with a short nail. The tip of her tongue slipped out between her teeth and hovered in one corner of her mouth.

"Oh, what the hell," she said, getting to her knees. Quick fingers undid the buttons on her work shirt, and moments later it lay on the grass beside the tablecloth. Slocum leaned forward and kissed her on the forehead. He slid his lips down past her ear, pausing long enough to nip it, then traced the curve of her throat as Lynn tossed her head back. Finding a breast, he took the nipple between his lips and began to suck. He felt her fingers in the curls at the back of his neck. He followed her down as she lay back, half on the cloth and half in the grass.

He opened his mouth and pulled more of her in, his hand cupping the other breast and teasing the nipple with his thumb. He heard Lynn breathe faster, and slid the hand down along her stomach. When it found the buttons of her jeans, it also found she had beaten him there: the buttons were already open.

She lifted her ass and arched her back while he pulled the dungarees down off her hips. Her legs thrashed for a moment, and then her boots were off. The denim followed.

"Your turn," she whispered, unbuttoning his pants. She tugged once and again. His cock, already hard, snapped to attention, and she grabbed it while he struggled out of his pants. Slocum let her breast slide away from his mouth and knelt between her thighs.

She bent her knees and opened her legs, arching herself toward him. He slid his cock inside, and she surprised him by slamming her hips hard against him, taking him all the way in with a single thrust. He lowered himself to his elbows and worked his hips, staring into her face as they moved faster and faster. Her fingers dug into his ass, pulling and pushing him, adjusting his rhythm and urging him on.

The sound of their coupling grew wet, her juices oozing out with every thrust of his stiffness. Then, when she sensed he was about to finish, she pulled him down and buried her face in his shoulder. When he came, she held him, her hands refusing to let him back away.

"Stay," she whispered. "Stay until you go limp. Then make love to me again."

Slocum nodded wordlessly. He felt himself beginning to get hard again as the cool air swirled around them. Slowly she moved, using her muscles to tease and provoke him, hips absolutely still. And when he had risen to the occasion, she let him lead this time, a dancer confident in her partner.

When it was over, she let him pull out and lay there on the ground, her hair tangled, beaded with sweat. He sat up and looked at her. Her full breasts, flattened against her ribs, the curve of one arched leg half concealing and half revealing the dense tangle of her bush, beaded with fluid of another kind, the full lips, slightly swollen with their passion—every part of her seemed to complement every other. If she were imperfect, it would take a sterner critic than John Slocum to discover the flaw.

6

Slocum saw the small figure pacing back and forth in front of the ranch house. Even at this distance, he recognized Lynn Dawson. Judging by her movements, a jerky strut with abrupt changes of direction, she was agitated, even upset.

He clucked to the horses and snapped the reins. They picked up their pace, the bouncing wagon shaking so much it rattled his bones. He gritted his teeth to keep them from cracking together. As the wagon closed on the house, she heard the racket and stopped pacing. Slocum saw her raise a hand to shield her eyes from the late-afternoon glare. When she recognized him, she began to run.

Slocum was still three hundred yards from the house when Lynn met the wagon. He called the horses to a halt and jumped down from the seat, glad to give his butt a rest from the constant slapping of the rough wooden seat. "What's the matter, Lynn? What's happened?"

Lynn was breathless from her race, and fell into his arms, gasping for air. She tried several times to speak, but her voice was an unintelligible rasp, squeezed out between breaths. She started to sob.

Slocum stroked her hair, staring helplessly at the top of her head. He wasn't used to displays of emotion, and Lynn's agitation made him uncomfortable. Not knowing what else to do, he patted her back, mumbling into her hair whatever came to mind. He was aware how foolish he sounded, but it seemed to have the desired effect. Lynn stopped sobbing and took several deep breaths in succession. When she was sufficiently composed, she gave a great sigh. "Thank God you're here, John. I'm so worried."

"What's happened. Are you all right?"

"I can't find Amanda. She's still not home from town."

"I'm sure she's okay. Maybe she had some trouble with the wagon."

"No, I know it's more serious than that. A mother knows these things. I can tell, I tell you."

"Now hold on, Lynn. Don't go off half-cocked. Let's just go on into town ourselves. We'll probably meet her on the way."

She looked at him for the first time, searching his face with those deep green eyes as if to see whether he was telling her the truth or just telling her what she wanted to hear. After thirty seconds of scrutiny, she still wasn't certain.

"Come on, Lynn," Slocum said, grabbing her around the waist and hoisting her up into the wagon. "Scoot over, I'll drive."

Slocum lashed the horses into a fast trot. The wagon bounced through the ruts in the road as he pushed the team on past the house and toward Twin Trees. He glanced at the house as they passed, wondering whether Lynn was right. The house looked so empty, he was afraid there just might be something to her fears. It looked abandoned rather than unoccupied. Part of that was the maintenance it needed, work he would be doing as soon as he finished stringing the wire, but part of it was a state of mind, Lynn's state of mind.

As they rushed on toward town, Slocum kept scanning the road ahead, looking for some telltale sign, a few curious birds, perhaps a cloud of dust signaling an oncoming wagon. But the road looked every bit as empty as the house had. He tried to keep himself from getting drawn into Lynn's near-hysteria, but it was not an easy thing to resist.

As the town drew closer, he could sense Lynn's rising tension. She moved closer to him, resting one hand on his leg. Her fingers seemed to gouge the flesh of his thigh more deeply as they got closer. So far, she hadn't said a word.

"Where was she going this afternoon?" Slocum asked. He wanted as much to break the tension as to elicit the information.

"Just to Kennedy's store. I gave her a shopping list. She was supposed to come right back. She knew that, and she always does what I tell her. That's why I know something must be wrong."

"You *don't* know that," Slocum snapped. "Quit trying to talk yourself into it."

Lynn lapsed into silence. Slocum wanted to tell her something that would comfort her, to convince her that there was nothing to worry about, but he was no longer so certain. He had fully expected to find Amanda on the way into town, the wagon with a broken wheel, one of the horses lame, maybe. But when they reached the outskirts and Amanda was nowhere to be seen, his confidence faded quickly.

Ignoring the scattered traffic in the dusty streets of Twin Trees, Slocum headed for the general store. He'd never been there, but the town was so small, he spotted the sign almost immediately.

The wagon lurched to a halt and Slocum jumped down, not bothering to tie the team off. He helped Lynn to the ground, then followed her into the store.

"Howdy, Mrs. Dawson. Amanda forget something?"

"No, no. I mean, I don't know. She was here already?"

"Oh, certainly. Big order you placed. I reckon this is Mr. Slocum? Amanda told me about him." The storekeeper watched Slocum as he spoke, and stuck out his hand after wiping it on his dusty apron. "Bob Kennedy," he said. "Pleased to meet you, Mr. Slocum."

Slocum took the offered hand absently. "How long ago did Amanda leave?"

"Two, three hours, I guess, why? Everything all right?"

"She hasn't come home," Slocum said. "We thought she might have run into trouble on the road, but there's no sign of her."

"Well, now, I don't think there's any need to get worried. She probably just took a little detour. You know how kids are. Can't never seem to keep their minds on their work."

"Amanda's not like that," Lynn snapped.

"Now, Mrs. Dawson, I didn't mean no harm, but it's a natural fact. Kids like to do things their own way, in their own good time. She probably just stopped off to see a friend."

"With a wagonload of supplies?" Slocum asked.

"Stranger things have happened, Mr. Slocum. I don't know how much you know about kids, but I got three of my own. I don't mind telling you, sometimes I think they do things just to get me upset."

"Those are *your* children, Mr. Kennedy. I know Amanda. She wouldn't do that. She's too responsible." Lynn was getting angry now, and Slocum realized that Kennedy had become a convenient lightning rod for her anxiety. She was so full of fear and nervous energy she had to let it out. The storekeeper was as good a target as any.

"No need to get all het up, Mrs. Dawson. I'll tell you what. Petey, my stock boy, knows Mandy. Let me ask him if he knows any place she might have gone. It can't hurt."

Lynn nodded but said nothing. She turned to Slocum, her jaw set in a rigid line. Her full lips had been compressed to thin white lines, all the blood squeezed out by the taut muscles in her face.

She turned away from Kennedy, sucking her cheeks in and chewing at their insides. When Petey appeared, she looked at Slocum and he took the cue.

"Petey, Mr. Kennedy here tells me you know Amanda Dawson, that right?"

"Yes, sir, I do. Her and me went to school together. Back when I went to school. I don't no more. She still does, I think."

"Okay, you think of any place she might have gone before going home this afternoon?"

"Gee, no sir. I don't think so. Amanda wouldn't do that anyhow, not with a wagon full of stuff."

Lynn sighed and shuffled toward him, her feet dragging the floorboards with a hollow scrape.

Outside, the sun was beginning to set, and the clouds were turning a dozen shades of blue-black and gray, shot through with pink and violet. Slocum looked up at the sky, realizing they had little more than an hour before dark. He waited by the passenger side of the wagon, then helped Lynn up into the seat. He walked behind the wagon and climbed into the driver's seat.

Taking the reins in his hands, he paused for a moment to look at her. "Any ideas?" he asked.

Lynn shook her head without answering. She turned to him, and he could see the fear in her eyes. Small pools of tears trembled at their corners, waiting for the last push. She wiped them away with the backs of her hands. "What am I going to do?" she asked, her voice almost inaudible.

"We'll find her, don't worry. There must be some simple explanation."

"It's those men, I just know it, those men in the wagons the other day."

Slocum had already started wondering whether there was any connection, but hadn't wanted to alarm her. It was the most logical explanation, but it was better if Lynn not dwell on it. "Probably not. They must be a hundred miles away by now. You scared hell out of them."

"I wish I had shot them dead."

"No," Slocum said, "you don't wish that. You're just upset. But you can't lose control. You have to hang on until we find her. There's no point in torturing yourself." Slocum trailed off because he didn't know how to finish his argument.

Lynn noticed. "Until we know for sure, that's what you're thinking, isn't it. Until we know for sure she's hurt, or..."

"Damn it, Lynn, stop it." Slocum grabbed her wrists and pulled her toward him. He started to shake her, knowing instinctively that it was the wrong approach. He caught himself, and just squeezed her reassuringly.

"I think we better go back to the ranch," Slocum said. "Maybe Amanda's there now. If not, we can decide what to do. On the way, I want you to check your side of the road carefully. You see anything unusual, wheel marks drifting off to the side, broken bushes, anything at all, we check it out. I'll do the same on my side. Okay?"

When she didn't answer, Slocum gripped her chin and turned her face up. "I said, 'Okay?'"

Lynn closed her eyes and shook her head almost imperceptibly. In a husky voice, she said, "Okay. Whatever you say."

Slocum cracked the reins, and the horses moved out. By the edge of town, they were under a full head of steam. Lynn held on to the side of the wagon with one hand to keep from bouncing around on the seat. "John," she shouted, "aren't you going too fast? I mean, how are we going to see anything if you don't slow down."

Slocum knew she was right, but his own anxiety was clouding his judgment. "Okay," he said, "you're right." He pulled back on the reins to slow the team to a medium trot. "I just wanted to cover the whole stretch before it gets dark." She seemed to accept that explanation and turned back to her side of the road.

As they headed home, Slocum spotted something every ten or fifteen yards, and every time they got closer, he could see it was a false alarm. Things taken for granted suddenly assumed significance. A snapped branch, a scrape in the dry earth, a newly broken rock—any one of them might be evidence of Amanda having left the road. And each time, he looked past the disturbance and saw nothing further, no second branch broken, no more scraped earth, the other rocks intact.

The shadows by the side of the road began to deepen as the sun set behind them. The vivid colors of the sky washed out, turning to grays and finally disappearing. Slocum kept hoping for something, some sign that Amanda had simply broken down and been forced to abandon the wagon, but as they drew closer to the ranch, his mood began to darken along with the sky.

He was thankful that Lynn, regardless of what she might be thinking, was keeping her own counsel. It would do no one any good if she were to panic. She was dangerously close as it was, and Slocum knew that talking about it would just throw fuel on the fire. This was one of those times when silence was the best tack.

The house came into view as the last rays of the sun speared through gaps in the cloud mass, bright blades of white light slashing across the sky, then winking off.

As night descended, Slocum noticed a pale glow in the front window. "Did you leave a lantern lit at the house?"

"No, why?"

"Because there's a light in the window."

"She's home, then. Oh thank God." Lynn clapped her hands and let herself cry without restraint. Slocum looked for the wagon, but it was nowhere in sight. He didn't want to point that out to Lynn, so he watched the house as they approached.

He braked the wagon in front of the house, and Lynn leaped down while it still rocked on its springs. She raced around in front of the horses and stomped onto the porch, calling, "Mandy, Mandy, we're here."

Slocum looped the reins and climbed down. He was just turning away from the wagon when he heard a piercing scream. He looked toward Lynn just as she collapsed onto the floor of the porch. Her head slammed into the floor-boards with a hollow thud.

Slocum raced to the porch and knelt beside her. She lay there moaning, and he glanced up when a flash of white caught his eye. Cradling her head, he let it down carefully, then stood up to snatch the paper pinned to the door with a hunting knife.

The childish scrawl, done in a blunt pencil, said, "If you want to see your dawter agen, we want slokum. Wate for an other not."

7

Lynn lay on the bed, curled into a tight ball. Slocum sat and watched her, unable to sleep, and knowing that she wouldn't sleep either. He cursed himself for bringing this trouble to her and Amanda. He knew it wasn't his fault, but there was no one else to blame—no one, that is, except the whiskey runners themselves, and they were out of reach for the moment. Slocum could only hope it wouldn't be long.

There was no question in his mind about whether or not to exchange himself for Amanda. He had no choice. And he knew that if he did have a choice, he would still go through with it. The world was cruel enough for adults; there was no need for its viciousness to intrude on children. And Amanda would soon enough have to face its harsher realities on her own. Childhood was too short as it was, and if there was anything he could do to protect what remained of Amanda Dawson's innocence, it was for damn sure he would do it.

His first instinct had been to get the sheriff and tell him what had happened. But deep inside, he knew that would be the equivalent of signing a death warrant for the girl. And when he added the fact that the less contact he had with the law the better off he would be, he dismissed out of hand whatever lingering thoughts he had.

This one was up to him.

He would meet them as they demanded. He knew that they weren't likely to be trustworthy, but here, too, he had little choice. If he didn't give himself up to them, they would kill the girl, he had no doubt. Whether they would let her go unharmed once they got their hands on him, he was far less certain.

So, for the moment, all he could do was to sit and wait for the instructions that would tell him where to go and when to be there. Lynn tossed and turned, and he felt the chill breeze through the half-open window. He grabbed a second blanket from the foot of the bed and wrapped it around her, tucking it under her shoulders and making a tight cone of wool around her legs.

Slocum walked to the window and looked out at the night. He turned the wick down, reducing the lamp's glow to little more than an ember. He walked outside and sat on the porch. It was getting cold, and the sky was a dark gray sheet. It looked like they were in for some cold weather. It was only a few weeks, give or take, before the snow started.

How quickly things can change, Slocum thought. A week ago, all he worried about was getting to Whitefish for another lousy job in an endless string of lousy jobs. Moving from place to place had become a habit. He wondered whether, if the opportunity to stay put for a while ever presented itself, he would know what to do.

Slocum walked to the corral. He leaned on the top rail and lit a cigarette. The little mare snorted, then crabwalked toward him, rubbing her side against the split rail fence. Slocum reached through to pat her on the rump. She whinnied, then moved away, turning her head to stare at him in the darkness. Slocum climbed the fence and turned to sit on the top rail. Hooking his heels in a lower rail, he puffed on the cigarette. A cold wind whipped around the corner of the barn, raising the hair on the back of his neck.

He watched the house with a touch of longing. For Lynn Dawson, it was a home, something he hadn't had in so long he wondered whether he ever did have one. The dim light in the window flared suddenly, smearing bright orange on the ground outside the house.

He saw Lynn's silhouette against the curtains. She seemed to be confused, starting first in one direction then disappearing on the other side of the window. The door banged open, and he heard her call him, an edge of hysteria in her voice. "John, John, where are you?"

Slocum felt guilty about leaving her alone, and he tossed the cigarette to the ground, landing on it with one boot as he jumped down from the fence. He called to her, and sprinted across the yard.

She stepped off the porch to meet him. "I got frightened," she said. "I woke up and didn't know where you were."

"I needed a little fresh air, that's all."

"I'm sorry you got dragged into this," she said. "It's all my fault."

"Look, you didn't drag anybody into anything. And if I wanted to ride out of here right now, you couldn't stop me. No one could. So stop blaming yourself. I'm going to see this thing through to the end. You'll have Amanda back in the morning, I promise."

She turned away to look at the dark sky that seemed to be slowly descending on the house, as if to crush it. "What about you?"

"What about me?"

"When will I have you back?" She folded her arms across her chest to keep off the cold.

"I don't know," he said.

"Never, you mean, don't you?" She whirled to face him, squeezing herself still harder with crossed arms. "You're not coming back, are you?"

"Good night," he said. He turned away and walked toward the bunkhouse. For a long moment, the only sound was his boots crunching on the earth.

"I know you're not," she shouted. "I know it." She started after him, then stopped suddenly, as if she'd run into a sheet of glass. "I know you're not coming back."

Slocum went into the bunkhouse. He fell onto the bunk without bothering to light the lamp. He was angry, not with Lynn but with himself. Angry because he couldn't answer her question. Angry because she represented everything he didn't have. And, especially, angry because he wanted to be able to answer her question and because he wanted to have what she had.

He stared at the ceiling, listening to the sounds of the night. It bothered him that he wasn't able to be more comfort to Lynn, but he had to look after himself first of all. He didn't know what the morning would bring. But he knew that if he were to have a chance to survive whatever might come, he would have to be totally and perfectly free. The least little encumbrance might slow him up. Not much maybe, but enough. What he didn't have might get him killed. Whatever future he might have with Lynn Dawson, or without her, depended on his rootlessness, his freedom from concern for others.

And he hated to admit it.

For a long time he listened, wondering whether Lynn might come to him. He was half hoping she would—and half hoping she wouldn't. To let his fate depend on her would be to relinquish whatever control he might have over his own destiny.

After a long time, he heard the screen door slam. He held his breath, waiting for her. When he counted to a thousand, then two thousand, and finally three, he realized she wasn't coming after all. The door had closed her in, not announced her coming out. Slocum sighed and closed his eyes.

It was cold in the bunkhouse, but he felt too drained to light a fire. It was easier to lay there, let the cold chew at him, burrow into his flesh, and work its way down to the bone. But the cold numbed nothing. He could still feel, and he didn't want to. He didn't want to feel anything. Attachments inevitably bred sorrow, and he'd had enough of that.

Lost in thought, he didn't recognize the sound at first. After several seconds of confusion, he realized it had been glass breaking. Slocum jumped up and ran to the door, dragging his gunbelt from the table. He draped it over his shoulder and held the Colt in his hand, stepping into the cold and slipping along the front of the bunkhouse.

A light went on in the house, and he sprinted across the yard, skirting the corral so closely he banged his ribs on the corner post. He lost his balance and stumbled forward a few steps before regaining control. Under the sound of his own feet, he heard the deeper bass of hoofbeats receding into the night.

On the porch, he noticed broken glass. He banged on the door, calling to Lynn to open up. When she did, she held a lamp in one hand and a ball of paper in the other. She handed it to him, and its weight told him it was the answer to his question. Wrapped around a rock, they had just received the final instructions for the morning exchange.

Slocum took the lamp from Lynn's hand and set it on a table. He cranked the wick up higher, then snapped the twine holding the paper and stone together. Smoothing the paper on the table top, he pressed the worst wrinkles flat.

In the same childish scrawl, probably written with the same broad-pointed pencil, he was instructed to meet Lavalle at the stand of box elders on the ridge, the same place the steer had been killed. He was told to come alone and unarmed. Any failure in this regard would mean that all bets were off.

They didn't spell it out, but they didn't have to. Slocum understood their type better than he cared to.

Lynn snatched the paper from the table and turned to him. "What's going to happen to my baby?"

Slocum didn't answer her. He didn't know. Instead, he took the note and crumpled it into a tight ball. Taking the chimney from the lamp, he stuck the paper into the flame and held it until it caught. He watched as the flames consumed the paper, leaving a thin, brown slip no larger than a postage stamp. He closed his fingers over the dying flame and crushed it out. He didn't feel anything.

Opening his fingers slowly, he saw the ashes and the bright red smear across his palm where the fire had seared his flesh. He felt Lynn's fingers clutching at his shirtsleeve, but he ignored her. Without a word, he walked back to the bunkhouse.

Morning wasn't that far off, and he had things to do.

8

Slocum was on the ridge by sunrise. He stood among the box elders, his eyes restlessly sweeping the shadows filling the valley on either side of him. The sun started as a red curve on the horizon, its bottom chewed ragged by the Little Belt Mountains to the east. It seemed to swell like a living thing, growing before his eyes. The deep, almost bloody red gradually brightened, turned orange, then seemed to explode in scorching yellow.

As it climbed higher, the sun spilled down into the valleys, sweeping away most of the shadow with its flood. The trees and taller rocks cast long dark fingers toward him, as if they were reaching out to touch him. As the sun continued to rise, the shadows shortened.

According to his pocket watch, it was nearly seven, and there was still no sign of Lavalle or his cronies—and, worse yet, no sign of Amanda. Slocum didn't like the naked feeling of standing on the ridge without a gun, but if one thing was certain, it was that Lavalle had not been kidding. If he found a gun on Slocum, Amanda Dawson was as good as dead.

As a man who kept himself alive by cunning and, more often than he liked, by brute force, Slocum felt vulnerable. He had thought about concealing the Colt in a boot or under his shirt, but finally dismissed it. He knew that if he needed a gun, he would need it quickly, and if it were concealed well enough not to be noticed it would also be difficult to get to in the split second he'd have to get his hands on it. A gun you can't get to is about as good as a small rock or a rotten tree branch in a fight. It was better not to risk it, especially since the risk was Amanda's as much as, if not more than, his own.

Slocum had ridden the mare and brought a second horse for Amanda. The animals seemed restless, alternately raising their heads to look around and straining at the reins lashed to a low-hanging tree limb. Slocum watched the animals carefully, thinking they might sense an approaching rider before he would. He wished he had binoculars. Seeing them at long range wouldn't help anything, but at least his nerves would have time to quiet down.

By seven-twenty, he started to worry that they had deliberately misled him. He wished he had thought to warn Lynn to stay indoors and keep a gun handy, but it was too late for that now. He bent to snag a handful of stiff grass and bunched it in his left hand. As he watched the valley below him, he lashed at his leg with the bunched grass, the tempo slowly increasing as his anxiety grew.

At seven-thirty, the horses spooked. They kept staring down into the western valley. Slocum turned his attention in that direction, but so far he saw nothing. A brace of quail suddenly exploded out of the tall grass just above the valley floor, followed a moment later by the brim of a man's hat, some fifty yards beyond the fleeing birds.

The lone rider picked his way carefully, keeping whatever cover the slope afforded between him and Slocum. The man didn't seem to be concerned that Slocum might not be there, and he didn't seem to care that Slocum might have a gun. His use of the cover seemed more instinct than design. Once or twice the rider glanced up at the crest of the ridge.

Slocum wondered whether someone across the valley

was watching him through field glasses. He knew he was in range of a Sharps or a Spencer. The big buffalo guns had a range of a thousand yards or more, and if someone wanted to kill him, he'd be an easy mark. He dropped to the ground and watched the approaching rider from behind the base of a tree.

Looking past the rider, Slocum searched for some sign that Amanda might be held nearby. But the lone rider appeared to be the only human being in the valley. As he drew closer, his features started to resolve. He was riding into the sun, and the shadow cast by his hat brim only covered his forehead. The man was clean-shaven, and appeared to be reasonably clean, so it couldn't have been either Lavalle or Jed.

There was, of course, the slim chance that the man had nothing to do with Amanda's abduction, but it seemed rather unlikely. The man was big and blocky. Slocum searched his memory but didn't recall seeing him the day the steer had been killed. He had probably been behind Lavalle in the small crowd. Things had been happening so fast at that point that Slocum hadn't been able to take in every face.

The man altered his direction slightly and now headed straight toward Slocum's horses. He seemed to know where they were, confirming the probability that they had been watching Slocum the whole time. He sat easily in the saddle, and Slocum admired his horsemanship. He controlled his mount, a big chestnut stallion, with little more than his knees and wrists. There was no sign of strain on the man's face, and he seemed perfectly relaxed and confident.

The rider was only fifty yards away when he pulled up. "Come on out, Slocum, I know you're there. Keep your hands up."

"Where's Amanda? Why didn't you bring the girl?"

"I said come on out. Don't give me a hard time. You don't have a prayer, cowboy. Come on out."

"And if I don't?"

The rider didn't answer the question. He backed off a couple of yards, then raised his right hand straight over his head. Slocum tensed, expecting to see several others come charging up the slope. Instead, a great, wet thud smacked at him from the left. A curious whimpering caused him to turn his head just as the little mare fell over. A second later the boom of a buffalo gun, like distant thunder, rolled up the grassy slope on the morning wind.

"Any more stupid questions, Slocum?"

Slocum climbed to his feet, still keeping himself concealed behind the slender tree. A real shot would have been able to hit either side of him, and he knew what the three- or four-hundred-grain slug of the buffalo gun would do to him. He felt a little silly hiding behind the frail tree, but it was better than nothing.

"I thought you were going to exchange the girl for me," Slocum said.

"You don't think we'd be dumb enough to bring her here, do you? Come on, I'll take you to her."

Slocum eased out from behind the elder and walked toward the horse he'd brought for Amanda. He glanced down at the mare. Her eyes were wide open, but there was no mistaking the dead glaze already shining in them. A few flies had settled on her lips, twisted open by the agony of her death. A gaping hole, turning brown against the buff-colored hide, had been torn in the back of her head. Slocum felt slightly nauseous, and choked back the bitter fluid churning in his gut. The little horse had been fond of him, and he of it. If he got out of this bind, somebody would pay for that mare, and it would be more expensive than just money.

He stepped past the corpse of the mare and grabbed the reins of Amanda's horse. The sudden sickening *splat* erupted not six inches from his left hand. The horse seemed to explode before his eyes for several seconds, as if it were happening in a world where time had slowed down. The horse staggered sideways, then its legs folded up beneath it and it seemed to collapse in on itself like a balloon suddenly empty of air.

Slocum jumped back. But this time, he knew to expect the thunder rolling up the slope.

The rider laughed. "Looks like you got to walk, cowboy." The man pulled a Colt Peacemaker from his hip and waved Slocum to step past him.

"How do I know you won't shoot me next?" Slocum asked.

"You don't, Slocum." He waved the pistol again, this time more vigorously. "Course, that wanted poster I saw ain't all that fresh in my mind. It *might* have said 'Dead or Alive.' If I knew for sure, you can bet your ass what it would be. But since my memory ain't what it used to be, you kinda lucked out."

Slocum started down the slope, his feet slipping on the dewy grass. Once, his heels went out from under him and he fell hard on the base of his spine. As he scrambled to his feet, he stole a look at the horseman. The guy was smart. He was hanging well back, and his eyes never left his prisoner. He let his horse worry about the footing.

Slocum debated making a quick rush at the rider, but he knew he'd never make it. And he'd bet a month's pay the buffalo gun was on him every step of the way. If he got himself killed, it would be the end of Amanda, too. They'd never let her go as long as she could identify them. But once they had him, they would bank on Amanda's silence, just as they had banked on his to keep Amanda safe.

As they neared the valley floor, a distant stirring, just a cluster of moving shadows in the brush marking a creek bed, caught Slocum's eye. The movement was slight, but it was more than the wind in the trees. It must have been Lavalle and Amanda and who knew how many more.

"You know, Slocum," the rider said, "that's a pretty little girl, that Amanda. You probably too busy pokin' her mama to notice, but some folks got a better eye than others." The man laughed, and Slocum balled his fists. His sense of vulnerability had turned into impotent rage. He wanted to answer, but he knew it would just encourage additional taunts.

"How is the old lady? Good as she looks? Them pants she was wearin' made her look pretty solid. Course, I like a woman with a little meat on her bones, know what I mean? But some of them boys got different ideas. I hope we're not too late to save little Amanda from a fate worse than death. Don't you?" he laughed again. "I like that. A fate worse than death. I seen that in a stage play once, in New Orleans. That little girl got away in the nick of time. Maybe Amanda will too."

Slocum stopped in his tracks and turned to face the rider. He calculated the angle between himself and the shadows he'd seen. If he was right, they wouldn't risk using the buffalo gun. The slug would pass right through Slocum and take out the rider, too. He moved so quickly, the man on the horse didn't know what to do.

He raised his Colt, but Slocum ignored it. He grabbed the man by the wrist and pulled him down until their faces were mere inches apart. Slocum hissed, "I'm warning you, mister, I find so much as a smear of dirt on that girl's cheek and you're a dead man. You understand me?" He twisted until something snapped in the rider's wrist, then flung the arm away like a butcher ridding himself of a chicken head.

"You son of a bitch . . ."

"Save it," Slocum snapped. He turned and walked on down the slope, picking up speed as he drew closer to the creek bed. He headed straight for the tall trees where he'd seen the movement. The horseman cursed him, but Slocum ignored it. He'd made his point. He stepped into the brush and let the branches snap back, keeping the rider at a distance. When he broke through the creek side of the brush, he stepped down into the shallow water. To the right, about ten yards away, three men sat on horseback. One of them cradled a Sharps over his saddle.

He grinned at Slocum. "Nice shootin', huh?"

"Where's the girl?"

The man with the buffalo gun looked at his companions. "Girl?" he said. "You see a girl? I don't see no girl. No girl here, cowboy." He laughed.

So that's how it was going to be, Slocum thought. His worst fears were confirmed. He started toward the man with the buffalo gun as a lone rider burst through the tree line and down into the creek. Slocum turned as he heard the horse continue toward him. But not soon enough. The rider swiped at him with the butt of a carbine. Slocum ducked to one side but lost his footing on the slippery rocks. He fell heavily. As he struggled to regain his feet, the buffalo gunner's companions leaped from their horses.

The man whose wrist he'd broken swung the carbine around and pointed it at Slocum's midsection. "Stay right there, asshole."

The blow took him by surprise. He saw the water sparkling in the sunlight. It caught fire and then everything went black. Slocum collapsed into the cold creek. The water almost immediately brought him back to consciousness. He spluttered for air as he felt his hands being twisted behind him. Then he felt the sharp cut of rawhide being twisted around his wrists.

His captors dragged him to his feet. The buffalo gunner looped a rope around Slocum's shoulders. "I hope you don't fall again, cowboy, 'cause I ain't stopping for nothing less than a miracle." He climbed onto his horse and snugged the lariat around his saddle horn. He kicked his horse into motion and headed down the creek bed. Slocum staggered along behind, half running and half falling. His feet kept sliding on the mossy stones in the creek bottom, and it was all he could do to keep himself from getting dragged off his feet.

They had gone about two hundred yards when they rounded a bend. Under a clump of trees, hitched and ready to roll, sat Lavalle's three wagons. The man towing him slowed up, then stopped, his horse still in the creek bed. The sudden shift sent Slocum sprawling into the water again. As he climbed to his feet, someone called his name. His ears were full of water, and he shook them free as the man called again.

"Mr. Slocum, how nice to see you again."

He turned and found himself staring into the bearded smile of Clyde Lavalle.

"Where's Amanda Dawson?" Slocum asked.

"Oh, don't bother yourself about that. She's well, I assure you. She's safe, and will remain so. As long as you don't try anything foolish."

"You were supposed to set her free when I gave myself up."

"So I was. But I'm a businessman, Mr. Slocum. When I realized just how valuable the young lady was, I knew that fortune had smiled on me yet again. And so soon after I became aware of *your* value to me. I could hardly believe one man could be so favored by the gods."

"Value? What value?" Slocum demanded. "You wanted me, you got me. Now let her go."

"But that would be foolish of me, Mr. Slocum. You see, Amanda, too, is worth money. It seems that her virginity will bring a high price in San Francisco. And I propose to realize that value, if at all possible." Lavalle winked. "But then, nothing is so perishable as virginity, eh?"

9

Slocum struggled to sit up. He had been bouncing around the bed of the wagon for several hours. His back and hips were killing him. The constant pounding of his body against the wooden floor of the wagon had battered and bruised him. He felt as if he'd fallen off a mountain. His hands were getting numb, since the circulation had been almost completely cut off by the rawhide. It had gotten wet when he fell into the creek, and as it dried, it shrank. Curling his fingers against his wrists, he could feel the puckered skin on either side of the thong.

The canvas cover was drawn shut across the rear of the wagon, but he could see the last reddish light of sunset through the imperfect closure. Exhausted by the morning ordeal, he had slept fitfully in spite of himself. The small caravan had not stopped for an afternoon meal. Slocum guessed Lavalle was anxious to put as much distance as possible between himself and Twin Trees.

Lynn Dawson was probably frantic. And she had almost certainly gone to the sheriff by now. He had told her to wait until noon. He hadn't wanted the sheriff sticking his nose in unless it was absolutely necessary. And he knew that Amanda would need her mother, so he didn't want to run the risk of Amanda showing up and finding no one home. But all that was just so much smoke now. Amanda needed the kind of help neither her mother nor the sheriff could give her. Slocum wondered whether he would be able to provide it. The odds didn't look too promising.

Whenever he had been awake, Slocum had tried to listen in on the conversation of the two men in the seat of the wagon. But the noise of the creaking floorboards and the sloshing of the whiskey in the stacks of barrels between Slocum and the front end of the wagon had drowned out all but scraps of banter. He had hoped to get some idea of where they were, or where they were headed. Anything he could learn would be useful information, when and if he managed to escape.

Slocum wasn't even sure how many men were in Lavalle's band. He had counted eight or nine the morning the steer had been killed, but there could have been more. Even if he went on the assumption that he had seen them all, the odds were too long for a man alone and unarmed. His first task would be to reduce those odds. But he couldn't even think about that until he freed his hands.

The wagon lurched suddenly to the left. The brakes squealed, and the wagon nosed down at a sharp angle. Slocum slid forward into the kegs, slamming his shoulder into the bottom row. He groaned, and his arm went numb for a moment. When the feeling returned, a sharp pain stabbed along his upper arm and halfway down toward his wrist. He tried to sit up, but the steep angle of their descent kept throwing him off balance. He stretched himself across the wagon, bracing himself against its sides with shoulder and heels. The angle made his neck throb, but it was better than slamming around the wagon bed like a side of beef.

The descent seemed to last forever. When the angle gradually flattened out, Slocum let himself slide free, relaxing the pressure of his feet against the wagon wall. His calves cramped, and his neck felt as if it had been impaled on a flaming sword. His arm, at least, was almost back to normal, the stabbing pain muted to an intermittent throbbing.

Rolling onto his stomach, he tried to relieve some of the pressure on his wrists, but the rawhide was so tight that it did little good. He was afraid of gangrene. Wriggling his hands as best he could, he sought an angle that would permit him to stretch the thong a bit to restore circulation. Gritting his teeth, he twisted his hands like the blades of a pair of scissors, pivoting on the spot where they met. The pain shot up toward his elbows, but he could feel nothing at all below the wrist.

It felt like an amputation with a rusty hacksaw, but he kept twisting. Gradually, he felt the leather begin to give way a bit. He stopped for a moment, then rearranged his hands. Making fists, he bent first one wrist and then the other. The rawhide stretched a bit more, but the lack of feeling in his hands made it impossible to tell whether he had stretched the binding enough. To be on the safe side, he repeated the scissors maneuver, then rested his hands, allowing them almost perfect immobility, lying in parallel one atop the other.

In a few minutes, he felt pins and needles in both hands. The tips of his fingers throbbed painfully, but he sighed with relief. As much as it hurt, at least he could relax a bit. The circulation slowly returned to normal. The immediate danger of gangrene was past.

The wagon had slowed to make the trip down, and it continued to travel at reduced speed even after reaching the bottom of its descent. He could hear the men in the front discussing something in low voices. There was an undercurrent of excitement in their conversation, but he couldn't make out the words. Suddenly, the wagon stopped.

In the abrupt silence, Slocum heard Clyde Lavalle bellowing orders to his men. The other wagons creaked to a halt, and he heard the squeak of a tailgate being lowered.

Heavy boots crunched on gravel alongside Slocum's wagon.

"I don't know, Clyde," a familiar voice said. "Them redskins don't look all that happy to see us."

"Leave it to me, Martin, I know what I'm doin'. The redskin who can resist my sales pitch ain't drawn a breath yet."

"Okay, if you know what you're doin', but I got a funny feelin' you're about to meet your match."

"You watch me. You got to remember, we ain't just carryin' firewater, we got fire*power* on our side too. You'd be surprised how powerful thirsty an Injun gets when he looks into a barrel fulla lead."

Martin laughed, and the feet moved on. A few moments later, Slocum could hear Lavalle call to someone, obviously the leader of a small band of Indians.

"Howdy, Chief," Lavalle began. "Nice little village you got here." The Indian responded in his native tongue. It was as alien to Slocum as it was to Lavalle.

"Now listen here, Chief, you got to talk English, you talk to a white man."

The Indian grunted, then said something else in his own language. The voice was muffled this time. Slocum guessed the Indian had turned to say something to one of his own men. Slocum shinnied on his butt to the tailgate of his wagon. He rolled over onto his stomach and got to his knees. The process took a couple of minutes. While he repositioned himself, Slocum listened to the conversation. Judging by the edge in Lavalle's voice, it was not going well for him. The Indian had compromised to the extent that he would answer in staccato English, mostly negative.

Slocum leaned his head over the tailgate and poked the canvas away by jerking his head to one side. He couldn't see anything but the back of one man's left side, but he could hear more clearly.

"You wait here," the Indian said.

"You got five minutes," Lavalle hollered. Slocum guessed the Indian had walked away to talk things over with his braves. While he waited, Lavalle mumbled a steady stream of expletives, most of which ended in "redskin" or "Injun."

"So much for your salesmanship, Clyde," Martin laughed.

"You shut the hell up, Martin. This ain't over yet."

"The hell it ain't," Martin said. "I can—" The rest of the statement was swallowed by a grunt. Suddenly, Martin pitched into Slocum's line of sight, skidding on his back. His lower lip was split open, and he reached up with the back of one hand to wipe blood away. He left a dark smear on his chin.

Lavalle's boots straddled the prostrate man. Slocum could see him from the knees down. "I told you to shut the fuck up. But you never listen."

"You're gonna do something like that once too often, Clyde," Martin warned.

"Not in your lifetime. Now get up!"

Martin scrambled to his feet as Lavalle backed away. The canvas slipped open a bit further, and Slocum saw two Indians in a clump of low underbrush. Just beyond it, a sliver of water reflected the last red rays of the sun. The Indians both carried carbines. The nearer of the two raised his left hand just above his head. A moment later, Slocum heard the chief return.

"Well, Chief, what did you decide?" Lavalle said, trying to sound amiable.

"No," the chief answered.

"No? What the hell do you mean, no? You can't turn down a deal like this. This is the best goddamned whiskey in Montana—and Wyoming, too."

"The white man's whiskey is no good for the Indian. It

just makes trouble. The Blackfoot have seen this trouble. We don't wish to see it again."

"Well, you damn well better. I got to sell this stuff to make a living."

"That is not my concern."

"That's what you think, Chief. You just better get ready to . . ." A symphony of carbine levers drowned out the rest of Lavalle's words. The two Indians Slocum had spotted stepped out of the underbrush.

"Holy shit!" Martin said. "These bastards aren't kidding. I think we better move it, Clyde."

"Shut your face. I'll decide whether to move, and when."

"You better decide quick, Clyde. I don't think the chief is all that patient a man."

"Listen to your friend," the chief said. "We don't want trouble. But we don't want whiskey, either. Please leave."

"It's kind of late in the day for us to be movin' on now, Chief," Lavalle said.

The chief said, "That is not my problem. Leave now!"

Lavalle agreed. "All right, all right. Hold your horses, Chief. We're leavin'." His boots appeared again, and Martin followed on his heels. "Don't you say a fucking thing, Martin," Lavalle snapped. "This ain't over yet."

"It ain't, huh? That's news to me *and* the chief."

A moment later, Lavalle shouted instructions, and the wagon began to move. The wagons moved slowly, like a kid dragging his feet on the way to an unwelcome chore.

It was dark now, and Slocum could no longer even see the slit where the canvas met unevenly. About an hour after sundown, the wagons stopped again. Slocum's wagon had pulled off at an angle, and he realized they were being formed into a tight triangle. Moving toward the tailgate again, Slocum pressed against the canvas to hear whatever he could.

Lavalle was addressing the men. He sounded angry. His speech was slurred, and Slocum guessed he had been drinking.

"Gonna make them redskins pay for this," he began.

As before, the man known as Martin put in his two cents. "I don't see that we ought to do anything foolish, Clyde."

"Shut up, Martin. We let them Blackfeet get away with this, won't be an Injun between here and the Pacific gonna buy from us. When you're in charge, you can make the rules. Until then, what I say goes. Anybody doesn't like it can tell me right now. I'm in the perfect mood to listen to that kind of shit."

Slocum heard mumbling, but nobody raised his voice to disagree or to challenge Lavalle. "All right, then," he continued. "I reckon there must have been ten men, twelve tops, in that camp. Head to head that makes us just about even."

"Even for what?" Martin wanted to know.

Lavalle ignored the question. "But we surprise them red buggers, it don't make no difference they got twenty, twenty-five. We can take 'em."

"You're not seriously proposing to start a war with those Indians just because they wouldn't buy the goddamn whiskey, are you?" Martin asked.

"War? Hell no. What war? Nobody said nothing about no war. All I said was we're gonna punish them bastards. Somebody finds a few dead Indians, ain't gonna make nobody upset. Unless they're other redskins." Lavalle laughed. He belched, and Slocum could hear the rumble in the big man's stomach as he nearly vomited.

He must have been hitting the juice pretty hard, Slocum thought.

When Lavalle continued, he was still swallowing, and it sounded like he was trying to eat his own words. "We can teach them bastards a lesson, and won't nobody but us know what happened."

"Suppose they're expecting us," Martin demanded. "You think they ain't watching us right now?"

"They're just Injuns, fer chrissakes, Martin, not gods or devils. They can be fooled just like anybody."

"You think riding in a big circle is gonna fool them?"

"You think it ain't? Besides, we roll down on 'em with that Gatling gun bangin' away, won't make no difference, will it?"

10

Slocum's wagon moved again, this time silently. He realized it had been unhitched from the team and was being
pushed by hand. When it stopped this time, the canvas
cover was ripped aside. Framed against the stars, a pale
light from the sliver of moon painting his face with deep
shadows, stood Wilbur Hartley, the man with the buffalo
gun. He fumbled with the pins and muffled the chains with
his free hand, leaning the Sharps against his left shoulder.
When it was unpinned, he lowered the tailgate, supporting
it with both hands to keep the squeak to a minimum.

He glanced at Slocum, a tight smile barely turning up
the corners of his thin-lipped mouth. "You awake, cowboy?"

Slocum didn't answer, and Hartley grunted as he
climbed into the wagon. Under his breath, he mumbled, "If
you ain't, you sure as hell will be the first time ole Arlene
barks." He patted the octagonal barrel of the big buffalo
gun the way a hunter pets a favorite retriever.

Hartley stretched out on the floor of the wagon, his feet
braced against the barrels in front. He cocked the big gun
and fiddled with the sights for nearly a minute. When he
was satisfied, he rested the Sharps on the floor of the
wagon, his arms folded across its top.

Slocum feigned sleep, narrowing his eyes to slits and
straining past Hartley to the floor of a broad valley. In the

faint light of the moon, he could just make out a creek shimmering among the trees like the trail of a giant slug, meandering its leisurely way eastward. Just to the right of center, a brilliant orange smear spattered with black cones seemed out of place. It was, Slocum realized, a small Indian camp. A dozen tepees, as usual oriented to points of the compass, formed a regular pattern of darkness against the light thrown by a huge bonfire at the center of the village.

For a long time, Hartley lay motionless on the floor. Slocum thought he might have fallen asleep. The man's breathing was heavy and contented, whistling through his nose like a grandfather's boozy snore. As the moon continued to slip across the sky, the angle of its light changed, and Slocum could see shadows dancing in a soundless rhythm as the man tapped his fingers softly on the breech of the Sharps.

Slocum shifted his weight, and Hartley turned to peer into the darkness for a few seconds. When Slocum didn't move again, he turned back to his silent survey of the valley floor. Like tiny sentries, a double row of cartridges for the Sharps stood on the lip of the wagon.

Tiny figures moved across the orange smear as the men and women of the Blackfoot camp went about their late-evening business. The traffic grew less and less frequent. A lone sentinel stood on the edge of the camp. In the farthest reaches of the light thrown by the flames, Slocum could see the Indians' horses. The animals were little more than dark patches in the orange-tinted fringes of the camp.

Hartley seemed to be focusing his attention on a particular spot, as if he were waiting for something specific, perhaps a sign. Slocum thought about shouting to warn the Blackfeet, but he doubted his voice would carry far enough. And he knew he'd get only one chance. At best he would be gagged for the duration, and at worst he would get his throat slit by the bone-handled skinning knife in a beaded sheath in the center of Hartley's back. And Amanda Dawson was out there somewhere, probably in one of the other wagons.

Slocum spotted a quick flicker of light far to the left of the camp. It baffled him for a moment, until he realized that someone had lit a cigarette. Hartley must have seen the light too, because he cursed under his breath. Slocum glanced at the sentinel, but if the Indian had seen the light, he gave no evidence of it.

The silence seemed to deepen as the moon began to slip lower on the horizon. It was just visible around the edge of the wagon cover. Slocum wondered whether Lavalle was waiting for the moon to set before making his first move. The quiet was beginning to get on his nerves. He wanted Hartley to forget about him, at least until he was ready for the first shot.

Slocum was puzzled by Lavalle's mention of a Gatling gun. The weapon was heavy, and it made no sense to carry it. A skillful counterattack would overrun the gun position in nothing flat, if the Blackfeet were smart enough to wait for the first ammunition drum to run out. Lavalle would surely know that. If he had the gun at all, it wasn't likely that he was unfamiliar with either its weight or its tactical limitations. That meant it was somehow mobile yet silent, something Slocum found hard to believe.

While he still had moonlight, he searched the valley floor for some sign of a wagon, the most likely way to keep the Gatling maneuverable. But how the hell could they have gotten the gun close enough to be effective without making enough racket to warn the Blackfeet?

Before he got a chance to find the Gatling, the moon slipped below the horizon. The campfire had been slowly burning out, and the orange circle had shrunk considerably.

The flames suddenly erupted as two dozen horses exploded across the center of the camp. The embers were kicked into a million tiny stars as the frightened animals charged right through the blaze. The uproar brought the Blackfeet charging into the open. The women scurried after the horses, while the men rushed into the darkness.

Hartley tensed as he picked up his Sharps. He sighted slowly, almost casually, the muzzle of the big gun sliding back and forth across the clearing. Slocum tensed his shoulders, silently drawing his knees back toward his chest. He lifted his boots above his head and brought them slamming down on the base of Hartley's spine. The Sharps went off as it slipped from the startled sniper's hands and clattered onto the floorboards. The neat rows of cartridges were knocked loose, and most of them rolled off the end of the wagon.

Quickly, Slocum raised his feet a second time, again bringing his heavy boots down hard on the thrashing assassin. The man cursed and rolled into a ball like an armadillo. He was trying to get out of the wagon without exposing his spine to a third assault. Using his arms, he dragged himself forward as Slocum struggled to his knees and pitched forward, landing on the surprised marksman with his full weight.

With his hands tied, Slocum would be defenseless if Hartley managed to break free. Unable to use his hands to hold on, he was tossed to one side as the pinioned man rolled to his left, slamming Slocum hard into the floorboards.

The Sharps slipped off the edge of the wagon, following the cartridges into the darkness. Hartley cartwheeled out of the wagon, landing on his back in the dirt. Slocum rolled toward the end of the wagon to fall on top of the gunner. He was brought up short by the glittering needle of the skinning knife hovering just below the wagon bed. Hartley had expected Slocum's maneuver. Had he completed it, he would have impaled himself on the slender knife.

Hartley cackled. "Got you now, you bastard." He scrambled to his feet, backing away from the wagon and dragging the Sharps by its muzzle. He twirled the gun as he stood upright, bringing it in a tight arc. Slocum saw it coming but was unable to get out of the way. The rifle butt caught him a glancing blow, stunning him for a moment. The Sharps had landed on his collarbone, and Slocum thought for a moment it was broken. He rolled away from the tailgate while Hartley hurriedly reloaded the rifle.

With a huge smile, Hartley turned the Sharps around. "Stay right there you sonofabitch, or I'll make a hole in you could swallow a horse. You hear me?"

"I hear you," Slocum said.

"Now get back here." Hartley said something else, but the Gatling gun had opened up, drowning it out. Slocum glanced toward the horrible chattering. Brilliant flashes marked the spot on a hillside above the camp.

Slocum eased forward, nervously eyeing the muzzle of the Sharps.

"Get your hands over the edge of the wagon, sport," Hartley snapped. Slocum did as he was told.

The man eased a pistol out of his belt and bent to place the Sharps on the ground. When the rifle was safely down, he stepped to the side of the wagon, keeping the pistol trained on Slocum's midsection. He tugged a coil of rope free, shook it loose, and found the free end. He slipped it between Slocum's wrists behind the rawhide, fed it through a slipknot at the other end, and jerked it taut.

Looping the rope over a sturdy tree branch, he hauled on the loose end, gesturing for Slocum to stand up. When the rope was tight enough to suit him, he lashed it to one wheel of the wagon. Slocum balanced precariously on tip-toe at the very lip of the wagon bed. If he were to try to get out of the wagon, he would hang suspended by his wrists, the rawhide cutting deeper into his flesh.

"That ought to hold you, cowboy," Hartley grunted.

Slocum could do nothing but watch as the man sat on his haunches and raised the Sharps to his shoulder. In the scattered fire below, figures danced back and forth. A sudden brilliant flash was followed by a noise like a thunderclap. In an instant, one of the tepees was torn to spiraling pieces by the stick of dynamite.

Hartley laughed, then grew quiet as he sighted in on his first target. After the dynamite, the rifle shot was almost quiet. In the heart of the camp a slender figure, an old woman, judging by the silhouette, fell to the ground as the report of the Sharps was swallowed by the thunder below. The Gatling continued to chatter intermittently, and Slocum realized that Lavalle was smarter than he had thought. The gun was firing only sporadically, making it impossible for anyone in the heat of the battle to know whether it was simply pausing or reloading. That uncertainty would prevent a charge.

A second tepee splintered across the clearing, and thick smoke began to hide the orange glow. In the chaos, the braves abandoned their plan to counterattack and turned their attention to the women and children. Hartley banged away at long range, as Slocum watched helplessly.

Suddenly, a half-dozen men on horseback charged into the center of the campsite, waving their guns and firing indiscriminately into the milling crowd. A third blast shattered another tepee, and the smoke gradually obscured Slocum's vision. Shadows faded in and out as they moved through the smoky pall. The firing seemed to reach a peak and then quickly fell away. The Gatling, notoriously inaccurate, had stopped as soon as the horsemen charged into the camp. As appalled as he was, Slocum had to admire the sophistication of Lavalle's plan.

After what seemed like an eternity, the firing stopped altogether. The shadows were nearly motionless now, clustering into a tight knot near the heart of the cloud of smoke. The wind ripped at the veil of smoke, tearing it into scattered rags and then to lace. The fire was still burning, but it had been so fragmented by the frightened horses that it was impossible to see any details.

Hartley stood up and leaned on his rifle. He backed toward Slocum, still keeping his eyes on the scene unfolding on the valley floor. "How 'bout that, cowboy? Ain't that somethin'? Old Clyde sometimes does more than talk, don't he?" He cackled again, this time letting it out of his gut. When he stopped, Slocum heard the laughter fade away into the trees and slide like an avalanche into the valley below.

The knot of shadows began to break up into two smaller clots. Watching it was like watching a river break in two around an island at its heart. The two separate streams coalesced and stood nearly motionless. Brilliant flashes sparked at the heart of one half of the shadow, and the other half collapsed in on itself.

Unexpected light bloomed suddenly around the edge of the camp, and Slocum realized the remaining tepees had been torched. The abrupt glare was like a sudden sunrise. In the brilliant light, Slocum saw the heap of bodies. Even at this distance, it turned his stomach. He turned his head to vomit, spewing his guts to one side. The terrible taste of it lingered long after he stopped wretching. Transfixed by the horror, he watched the survivors mount up and wave their hats in the air like graduating schoolboys.

They started up the slope, heading toward the wagons.

Just before they passed out of the circle of flame and were swallowed by the darkness, Slocum saw a slender figure stumbling at the end of a rope. He wondered whether the woman wished she were dead.

He knew that before long she certainly would.

11

Slocum watched the procession climb the slope. The eerie glow cast by the burning camp made the scene a tableau from hell. Starkly outlined against the flames, still partially wreathed in smoke, Lavalle and his men wound up the face of the valley. A single horseman hung back, continuing to pull his prisoner by the rope.

The first to reach the ridge line was a small caisson pulled by a single horse. Slocum now knew how they had maneuvered the Gatling gun. As it pulled up near the wagons, he could see the hubs, thickly wrapped in rags, bleeding shiny grease to keep down the noise. Lavalle and five others on horseback arrived a few moments later. They were boisterous, flushed with victory.

"One drink, you bastards, that's all. I mean it, now," Lavalle barked. "Soon's Jed gets here with the squaw, we move out. No point in hangin' close."

The men dismounted and moved out of Slocum's sight. He could hear the sound of wood on wood, then a sudden splash as the keg's head caved in. One of the men ran off and reappeared a moment later with a battered dipper. "This ought to do it," he shouted. The announcement was met with a loud cheer.

Lavalle himself stood to one side, watching. He looked at Slocum once or twice, his face an immobile mask. Slocum couldn't figure him. He seemed smart and stupid, cruel and humane, a mass of contradictions. As if reading Slocum's mind, he walked close to the wagon where Slocum still stood on tiptoe, his arms ratcheted tautly above his head. His shoulder sockets felt like they were full of molten metal.

Lavalle sprawled on the ground under a tree, leaning his back against its trunk. He watched Slocum silently for several minutes. The sound of the drinking party abated quickly as the men finished their drinks and turned their attention to the departure.

"So, Mr. Slocum, what *are* you wanted for, anyhow? I ain't seen the poster, and Ralphie don't remember. Ralphie ain't interested in such details. He knows about the money, and that's the only reason it stuck with him."

Slocum made no answer, but it didn't seem to bother Lavalle. The big man pulled on his beard, for all the world a contented family patriarch indulging his grandchildren in a favorite game. "You know," he continued, "some things you never lose, you never forget. You see how we took out that camp? We done the same thing in '64, down to Tennessee. Only that time it was some rebs. My commanding officer, Captain Lucius Anderberg—Lucius T. Anderberg, to be exact—figured out how to take them. I done pretty much what he done then. It still worked. Course I added a few refinements of my own. That caisson, that's my idea. Used it with General Crook back in Dakota once or twice."

"Why are you telling me all this?" Slocum asked.

"Hell, I don't know. Who else am I gonna tell, them?" Lavalle pointed to the others with his bearded chin. "Like talkin' to a wall, talkin' to them. Little better than draft horses, the whole passel of 'em."

"What makes you think I'm different?"

"You're here, ain't you? You showed up. You must have known there was a chance I wasn't gonna release the girl. But you showed up. That takes courage. More than courage, Slocum. That takes heart. You got it. I got it. Ain't too many others got it."

"Why didn't you release the girl?"

Lavalle inhaled deeply and held the air in his lungs for a long time. When he let it out, it was with resignation. "Most men don't see past their noses, Slocum. These fools are like that. You want to lead men, you got to recognize that. Once in a while, you got to let them do something they want to do. Now take Martin, for example. He's a troublemaker, but he does what I tell him, long as I let him have his way now and then. He says we can get money for the girl in Frisco, we're goin' that way anyhow, and he feels like he's a little bigger than the others 'cause it was his idea. It don't cost me nothin', so why not?"

Slocum laughed. "You got a lot of nerve to talk about heart, Lavalle. Heart, courage, whatever it takes to let a fifteen-year-old girl go back to her mother, you don't have a lick of it."

Lavalle smiled. "Now, see, there you go. That's what I mean about you, Slocum. You say what's on your mind. See, standin' there on tippytoe like that, hands tied, most men wouldn't say what you just said. I admire that in a man."

"You didn't answer me, though," Slocum reminded him. "Where's your courage? You let a young girl suffer to keep an asshole like Martin happy? Seems to me you got a twisted idea of courage."

Lavalle climbed to his feet. He sighed again, then approached the wagon. "You may be right, Slocum. You just may be. Then again, you're tied up and I ain't, so who knows?" He shrugged his shoulders and turned away to look at the burning camp below. With an abrupt twist of his upper body, he turned and slammed a huge fist into Slocum's gut. As he walked away, he said, "See what I mean?"

Then he was gone.

On the slope, Slocum could make out the final horse-man, leading his solitary prisoner. It was too dark to see her clearly, but her graceful movement, even under the cir-cumstances, suggested she was a young woman. Outlined against the orange light, she appeared to be tall and slim. Her hair, in twin braids, slapped her shoulders as she struggled to keep her balance under the insistent pull of the rope. Her hands were tied in front of her, and she kept them wrapped around the rope to lessen its sawing at her waist.

The horseman reached the ridge, and Slocum recog-nized Jed. His arrival was greeted by hoots and catcalls from the others. Jed was grinning from ear to ear. Even in the semidarkness, his eyes shone with a drunken glaze. A cigarette dangled from one corner of his mouth, and Slo-cum guessed it was Jed who had stupidly struck a match just before the assault on the camp.

Lavalle approached him, standing with one hand on the reins. Slocum couldn't hear the whispered conversation, but Jed didn't look happy. He kept glancing toward Slocum then down at his boss. He shook his head violently, and Lavalle shifted his grip, grabbing Jed's thigh in his huge right fist and squeezing.

"Cut it out, Clyde," Jed whimpered. The others laughed and Jed swiped at Lavalle's head with one hand. Lavalle caught the hand with his own left and jerked backward using nothing but his left arm. Jed swung up and out of the saddle, his feet catching for a moment on his stirrups be-fore he catapulted over Lavalle's head and landed roughly on the ground.

Jed curled into a ball and lay there whimpering. Lavalle hauled him up by the collar and set him on his feet. "Now," Lavalle said, "you do like I told you."

Jed backed away, feeling behind him with one hand

until he encountered his horse. Then he turned, unlooped the lariat from his saddle horn, and jerked the rope sharply. The young woman went sprawling in the dirt, and Jed jerked the rope again. "Get up. Get the fuck up," he shouted. He tightroped along the edge of hysteria as he jerked the rope repeatedly while the young woman tried to rise.

Lavalle stood to one side, shaking his head as if to say "I don't know what's gotten into kids these days." Finally, he took a step forward and grabbed Jed around the waist. "*Let* her get up, for Chrissakes."

Jed stopped jerking the rope long enough for the woman to get to her feet, and Lavalle relaxed his grip on Jed's shoulder. Pulling again, this time less vehemently, he led her to Slocum's wagon.

He looked up at Slocum, and there was no mistaking the anger glittering behind the glaze in his eyes. He turned his back and loosened the rope around the woman's waist. He let it drop to the ground, and she stepped out of the loop. Her hands were still tied, but she did her best to rub away the pain of the chafing lariat.

"Get over here," Jed hissed, stepping up to the wagon. He glanced at Slocum again, his face a twisted grin. A small strand of drool on his chin glistened yellowly in the firelight. Jed grabbed her shoulders and pulled her toward the wagon when she didn't move fast enough to suit him. He spun her around and stepped in behind her. Reaching around, he cupped her breasts roughly, squeezing them through her buckskin dress. Slocum watched helplessly. The young woman bit her lower lip but wouldn't give Jed the satisfaction of crying out.

Disappointed, Jed let his hands slide down her rib cage and close around her hips. "Get up there," he said, grunting as he lifted her toward the wagon bed. Anxious to get away from her tormentor, she used her hands to scramble into the wagon.

"Cut Slocum loose of that rope while you're there, Jed," Lavalle hollered. "We got to git movin'."

Jed looked over his shoulder at Lavalle and cursed under his breath. "I ain't no damn slave, you fat fuck." But he did as he was ordered, stepping around the side of the wagon and untying the rope. When it was free of the wagon wheel, he tugged it off the tree limb and tossed it into the wagon. Jed closed the tailgate while Slocum tried to relieve the agony in his shoulder sockets.

He sat down on the floor, twisting his upper body as Jed disappeared. As he worked the joints loose, he suddenly felt hands on his back. Expert fingers began to knead the flesh around the tormented joints. Slocum was surprised. He turned to the young woman, who did not look at his face. She was intent on her ministrations, and her features were stony and cold.

"Thank you," Slocum said. "You don't know how good that feels."

The Indian woman did not respond. She seemed to be searching through the muscle and the cartilage to find the source of the pain. Her fingers were strong and hard, probing like medical instruments rather than human appendages. Harder and harder she pressed, deeper and deeper into his aching muscles. When she found what she was looking for, she concentrated her efforts on the pinpoint, firmly massaging with the very tips of her fingers.

A quick flurry of activity culminated in a lurch of the wagon. They were the last wagon in line, and as they rolled past the campfire, Slocum saw Lavalle pour a bucket of water on the flames. A great hiss of steam rose into the air and disappeared in the returning darkness.

Lavalle mounted his horse and kicked it into a fast gallop, passing the wagon on his way to the front of the small caravan. With nothing else to do, Slocum closed his eyes. A single rider had fallen into line behind the wagons, making sure the captives stayed put.

The woman lay down on the floor alongside Slocum. He glanced at her just as she closed her own eyes. In the cramped quarters, their bodies touched along their lengths as the wagons bounced from side to side. Slocum was acutely conscious of her, but he tried to push her supple body out of his mind. There was too much else to be concerned about. He couldn't afford to let himself get distracted.

He slept fitfully, waking whenever the wagon took a particularly violent bounce. Each time, he stared out over the tailgate, and each time, the tail rider was right behind the wagon.

After three hours, the wagon slowed and finally squeaked to a halt. He lay there in the darkness, every sense alert to whatever slim chance might come his way. After fifteen minutes, the woman stirred. She raised up on her hips and bent toward him. He felt her lips on his ear.

"Untie the laces on my dress," she whispered.

"You speak English?" Slocum said.

"Doesn't everybody?" she whispered. "Be quiet and do as I say." She rolled onto her right side. Slocum faced away from her. He groped along her hip, then wriggled to go still higher, for the knot on the rawhide lace. It was difficult working in the dark, more difficult still working with tied hands. The rawhide kept slipping away from his fingernails. She wriggled further over, almost on her stomach, to give him a better angle.

"Hurry," she hissed.

"I'm going as fast as I can, lady. Besides, I don't see why you want your dress off. These aren't the best circumstances for getting acquainted."

She ignored him. Finally, his nails bit into the knot

enough to loosen it. He pulled the loop slowly, careful not to lose his grip. Reluctantly, the knot opened. He felt like shouting when he felt the loose ends of the lace dangle freely against the back of his hand.

"Keep going," she whispered. "All the way down."

Slocum worked at the lace, pulling it eye after eye through the seemingly endless series of holes along the length of the dress. When the lace was free at last, the woman rolled onto her back. He turned to see her open it, the soft, beaded buckskin opening onto a softer, more opulently beaded skin. Magnificent breasts, their dark areolae just visible in the dim light, rose and fell as the woman panted from her exertion. Small jewels of perspiration ran down the taut slope of her belly and collected in her navel, where they captured the available light and seemed to send it back magnified a hundredfold.

She rolled on her stomach, and Slocum breathed a sigh. He wasn't sure whether it was of regret or relief. Her hands were now pinned under her.

"Pull the dress away, quickly."

Slocum lay back down to do as he was told. He couldn't see what he was doing, but the cool skin over taut, warm flesh was almost more than he could bear. When the buckskin was out of the way, she said, "Put your hands on me."

He did as he was told. His hands came to rest on a full, round cheek of her ass.

"Over and higher."

His fingers groped across the tight skin, descended into the cleft between her cheeks and then climbed toward the small of her back. Suddenly, where he least expected it, he found yet more buckskin and, beneath it, an unyielding stiffness. He didn't need to be told anything more. He groped around until he found the hilt of the small knife and drew it free.

The woman rolled onto her back again. She snatched

the blade from his hands and it disappeared. A sharp thud on wood was followed by a whispered severing as she cut the rawhide binding her hands. Slocum turned to face her, but she was as impassive as he had been earlier.

Holding the knife under his nose, she hissed, "Turn around."

At first, he resisted the order, thinking she meant to stab him in the back. He'd be damned if he'd make it any easier. When she hissed again, he grudgingly complied. A second later he felt the knife slip between his wrists. The rawhide parted quickly, and his wrists were free for the first time in nearly twenty-four hours.

Slocum sat up and rubbed his wrists vigorously. The woman, still naked, was on her knees. His eyes lingered on her skin, taking in every inch of her magnificent body. She sensed it, as if his eyes exerted palpable pressure on the full breasts and broad hips.

"Don't even think about it," she said. But she was smiling.

12

Slocum crept to the tailgate and peered out into the night. Blue Lake lay beside him, her head just below the tailgate. The sentry sat motionless on the ground, a carbine between his knees, butt down. A cigarette dangled from the guard's fingers, a thin plume of smoke coiling into the leaves over his head.

"Is he awake?" Blue Lake whispered.

"Yes, but not for long." Slocum watched as the guard took a drag on the cigarette, then dropped the butt on the ground. He raised the rifle and ground the butt into the dirt with the rifle's stock. Letting the rifle slip to the ground, he raised his hands high over his head and opened his mouth. A silent yawn contorted the man's features as he gave Slocum a good look at a mouth full of broken, brown-edged teeth.

Slocum ducked his head below the top edge of the wagon, cradling his head on his forearms. In the quiet, he could hear Blue Lake's breathing, her short, shallow gasps sibilant in the darkness. He could barely see her face in the pooled shadow of the wagon bed.

He shifted his weight and draped one arm across her shoulders. Pulling her close, he pressed his lips against her ear. She started to twist away, but he whispered, "Listen, we have to talk."

Blue Lake stopped struggling, but twisted her head

away from Slocum's mouth. "I can hear well enough," she whispered.

When Slocum said nothing, she moved closer. "I'm waiting," she said.

Slocum sighed. "They have another prisoner."

"He'll have to take care of himself."

"She's fifteen years old," Slocum said.

"Oh. I see."

"Yes." Slocum didn't know what else to say. He thought she should know, but he also knew that her knowing would change nothing. Their options were as limited as they were before. In the silence, Slocum could feel his nerves humming like electric wires. He wanted to move, to run, to lash out. But he could do nothing. Nothing but wait, and the waiting was killing him. To have something to do, he raised his head again to look at the guard.

The sentry was still awake, but as Slocum watched, the man's head bobbed toward his chest then snapped back. He looked around, as if he had heard something, then relaxed. Again, his head began to nod slowly toward his lap. Slocum lowered his head again. To wait again.

"Is she a relative?" Blue Lake asked.

Slocum sensed that she was talking to relieve her own tension. He shook his head. Then, when he realized she couldn't see him, he said, "No. The daughter of a friend."

"Still, you will have to leave her. Or stay here with her. They are too many for us to try to rescue her."

"I know." Slocum lapsed into silence again. He wanted to check the sentry, but thought it more important to regain control of himself. Too much was at stake for him to be reacting. He had to take charge of events, control them instead of being controlled by them.

Blue Lake solved his dilemma when she raised her own head. She peered intently for several seconds. She held her breath to still her own body, the better to detect the slightest motion of the guard. Slocum lay on his back and stared up through the back of the wagon. The stars were a brilliant blue-white. At random, they seemed to pulse in time to the beating of his heart, one waxing while another faded to black.

Intent on the heavens, he was taken by surprise when Blue Lake kissed him, a quick brush of her lips on his. Her mouth was hot, despite the coolness of the night air. Instinctively, he reached up to hold her to him. He expected her to pull away. Instead, she kissed him again, this time letting her tongue slide into his mouth. Drawing away, she whispered, "Let's move away from the opening."

Slocum slid toward the front of the wagon. As he turned to her, Blue Lake rose on her knees and untied the canvas flaps and closed them. The wagon was pitch dark. He heard a slight hissing and screwed his face into a puzzled mask. When Blue Lake knelt beside him and leaned over, he reached out to place a hand on her hip. He knew then that the sound had been the buckskin sliding over her skin as she removed her dress.

"You are very nervous," she said. "That is not good." She bent again to kiss him. He felt her braids brush across his face as she leaned close again. "We shall have to be quiet," she whispered.

"I promise," Slocum answered.

Her fingers undid the buttons on his dungarees. He arched his hips to let her draw them down and off. The anxiety left him limp. When her hands closed over his cock, she laughed. "You are not like an Indian," she said. "We always make love before a battle. Each time might be the last time. Even the first."

She began to stroke him, her fingers working the length of him, squeezing tightly until she reached the head, then back down to the root. She worked slowly, almost clinical in her detachment. There was not the least hint of passion in her action. Slocum felt himself begin to respond. A sharp crack outside the wagon brought them up short. Slocum listened intently, acutely conscious of the motionless hand on his cock, which had gone limp again.

When the sound died away, Blue Lake bent forward to whisper, "Perhaps this might help."

Her lips caressed the head of his cock, while her tongue twirled its slick heat around it. She took him in partway, her mouth closing gently. Her tongue continued to work as her teeth nipped at him. Slocum felt himself beginning to stiffen again, and Blue Lake took him deeper into her mouth. Slowly, she began to move her head up and down, each time taking him a little further in. Her slow, steady rhythm was having the desired effect.

Slocum reached under her to take her breasts in his hands. They were small but full. He couldn't help but remember Lynn Dawson, the feel of her larger, fuller breasts. He felt a twinge of guilt. Blue Lake must have sensed it, because she started to move her head faster. Her nipples grew hard against his palms, and he slid his hands along her ribs, keeping his thumbs against the hardness.

Blue Lake drew him still deeper, and he could feel the head of his erection pressing against the back of her throat. Her tongue seemed to swell with the gentle pressure. Sliding his hands still further back, he caressed the back of her neck. He wanted to take her head in his hands and seize control of her rhythm. When he moved higher, to tangle his fingers in her hair, she let him slip out of her mouth. The cold air on his wet shaft sent a shiver up his spine.

"Don't interfere," she warned him, her whisper sharp in the quiet.

She plunged forward again, swallowing him whole. This time, she moved her head more rapidly. He continued to swell as she worked faster and faster. He felt his muscles contract in that last instant before exploding. Blue Lake noticed it and stopped.

She took him in her hand and stroked him, her hands a different kind of warmth. She pumped faster and faster. Slocum could hear the moistness in her palm, the sticky gurgling of her saliva as she jerked him into a frenzy. A hundred bubbles formed and burst, tingling along the length of his cock. He arched his hips and reached for her, trying to bring her head back down, but her back stiffened. She stroked still faster, and he came in a spasmodic shuddering. He felt himself spurting into the darkness, the cold, sticky drops showering over his stomach and thighs. She let go, and his cock stood there alone, hard and quivering as he continued to twitch for several seconds.

Then, with a swiftness that amazed him, she swung a leg across his waist and took him in her hands again, squirming toward him until, with a swift jerk of her hips, she took him deep inside her. She lowered herself without restraint, letting the weight of her body carry her all the way down. She straddled him without moving for several seconds.

Blue Lake leaned forward, and Slocum felt a nipple brush against his lips. He opened to draw it in, his tongue twirling against the hard button. He sucked the breast in like a thirsty man drinking water in the desert. Driving his hips upward, he tried to penetrate to the very heart of her. Her hips rose with him. He drew back for another thrust, and she slipped sideways. His cock slid out, and the sudden cold made him shiver. He could feel the hair of her bush tickling the head of his cock and, just beyond, the thick moist lips, but she rolled to one side.

"That's for later, *after* we get out of here," she said. Slocum cursed under his breath, angry and, at the same time, admiring the ploy. She knew there wasn't much he wouldn't do for the chance to finish what she had started.

As his erection shrank in the cold, she reached down and took it in her hand again. Gently, she stroked him again, her fingers making that same wet, sucking sound.

"I'm sorry," she said.

"Sure. Sure you are," Slocum said without bitterness.

"Really, I am. But everything has a purpose and a time. If we get out of this, we *will* finish. *I* promise."

She let him drop, then playfully cupped his balls in one hand, kneading them with gentle fingers. Slocum began to wonder who really held him captive. Lavalle seemed almost incidental beside Blue Lake's clever manipulation of his mind and his body.

13

While Slocum waited for the sentry to fall asleep, he watched the sky. The bright stars had faded to a dull white, then started to disappear altogether. An overcast moved in, and soon the sky was a solid sheet of slate gray.

Blue Lake seemed content to sit in a corner of the wagon. Slocum admired her patience but had none of his own. He drummed his fingers silently on the floorboards, whispering under his breath, "Come on, you bastard, sleep. Sleep, you son of a bitch. Sleep, damn it!"

It was too dark to read his pocket watch, but Slocum put the time at somewhere around three A.M. The guard had been motionless for nearly twenty minutes, and Slocum knew it was now or never. He slipped over to Blue Lake and whispered it was time to go. When she didn't move, he took her by the shoulder and shook her gently. The sleeping woman stirred, and Slocum bent close to whisper, "It's time to go."

He edged back to the end of the wagon and stood up. It was a good drop to the ground, but he couldn't risk lowering the tailgate. The rattling chains and the squeak of old hinges were just too dangerous.

Slocum reached up and grabbed the last hoop supporting the wagon cover. He pulled down to test its strength and, satisfied, took a secure grip with both hands. Hauling himself up toward the canvas, as if on a chinning bar, he bent his arms against his weight. He lifted his legs up and out over the tailgate, hanging suspended from his aching arms.

Slowly, he lowered his feet toward the ground, then let his arms relax. At full extension, he was still nearly two feet off the ground, but there was no other way. He let go of the hoop and dropped to the ground with a whisper of stiff grass. His boots thumped on the hard ground, and he nearly lost his balance. Grabbing the top of the tailgate to steady himself, he held his breath without even turning around.

When he was certain the guard was still asleep, he reached up for Blue Lake. She leaned out over the tailgate and took his hands. Wordlessly, she pulled him closer, then, with the grace of a cougar, flipped herself up and over, tucking her legs in to avoid kicking the canvas roof of the wagon. She landed softly in her buckskin moccasins. Back to back, they stood for nearly a minute.

Blue Lake stared at the sleeping guard, alert for the slightest movement. When there was none, she relaxed and stepped away, allowing Slocum to turn. He held a finger to his lips and gestured that she should stay put. Moving slowly, carefully placing each foot before moving the other, Slocum covered the twenty yards in an agonizing slow motion.

When he reached the tree against which the guard slept, he continued on past, then doubled back in from behind the tree. He reached down for the carbine. It lay in the grass alongside the guard, just beyond his fingertips. Painstakingly, Slocum slid the gun toward him, until he could grab it securely in the middle.

With the carbine in hand, he moved quickly, stepping around the tree. He swung the heavy rifle like a club, catching the guard on the right temple. The wet thud sounded like a pumpkin splitting open. He waved Blue Lake forward, and she moved swiftly, her feet soundless in the grass. She stood in front of the unconscious guard, then knelt. Slocum saw the hand at the last second, intercepting its tight arc with a desperate lunge. He squeezed the slender wrist, forcing the arm back.

In her hand, Blue Lake held the small knife they had used to free themselves.

"No," Slocum hissed. "You can't."

Blue Lake struggled to free her hand, twisting the wrist until the point of the blade grazed Slocum's forearm. With a sudden jerk, he bent the arm back and the knife fell to the grass. Blue Lake was fast, but Slocum was faster. He slammed the butt of the rifle onto the knife handle, pinning it to the ground and leaving her nothing but the blade to grab.

"They killed my family," Blue Lake said.

"I know, and I'm sorry. But if you kill him, they might take it out on Amanda. As it is, they're going to be furious that we got away. Now let's move."

"No! Not until I get my revenge."

"You'll have it. But not now. All right?"

She said nothing, and Slocum asked again, "All right?"

She nodded, then her head collapsed onto her chest. It was too dark to see clearly, but Slocum still held her wrist. He could tell by the spasmodic tremors that she was crying. Slowly, he let go of the hand, first relaxing his grip a little, then when she made no attempt to snatch it free, letting it go altogether.

Slocum reached out to place a hand on her arm. Wordlessly, he squeezed. Her hand grabbed his wrist, and he thought for a moment she was going to try again to get the knife. Instead, she patted his hand, then stroked him as if to say she was sorry.

Slocum unbuckled the guard's gunbelt. He tugged it free and draped it over his shoulder. "Let's go," he said, standing up.

"What about horses?"

"Too risky. We get caught, they'll kill us for sure." Slocum stepped away from the tree, and Blue Lake followed. They moved as quickly as they could, limited only by the need to remain silent. They paralleled the streambed along which the wagons had traveled.

When they had gone about a mile, Slocum stopped so abruptly Blue Lake slammed into him. She nearly fell, and he caught her by the arm. "Sorry," he said.

"Why did you stop?"

"I think we better decide what we're going to do. How well do you know this country?"

"Well enough."

"What do you suggest?"

"Do I hear correctly? Is a white man asking a squaw what he should do?"

"That's right, and you better have some good ideas."

"Or?"

"Or we're going to be in big trouble."

"I think we should return to our camp."

"What for? It's been destroyed. Everyone is dead."

"Because I can't leave the bodies there to rot. Because my mother is one of those bodies. Because I have to. And mostly because I don't know what else to do."

Her bravado was gone as quickly as it had surfaced. She started to sob, and Slocum took her in his arms. He caressed her back, holding her close. His body quaked with the desperate energy of her sobbing. He wanted to absorb it, to soak it all up, take it into himself to rid her of it. But there was no way he could. The loss was hers. The horror of the slaughter was hers. The strewn corpses belonged to people she knew. They belonged to her, not to him.

In a way, Slocum envied her. It made no sense, he knew, except that it meant she had had someone to care

about, someone to care about her. It had been so long since
Slocum could say the same, he couldn't even remember
what it was like. But Blue Lake's pain, as fearful as it was,
made something else clear to him. He could see the other
side of the coin, the joy that could be shared by people who
cared for one another. It was at times like this, when the
pain is too great for one person to bear alone, that friendship and kinship matter most. Blue Lake had no one. No
one but him.

And he thought of Lynn Dawson, who also had no one.
No one but Amanda. And he knew that he was going to get
Lynn's daughter back to her safely or he was going to die
trying. He was still circling his hands across Blue Lake's
back, but he was so absorbed in his own thoughts he didn't
realize that she had stopped crying. She reached up to
touch his face. He felt her cool fingers on his cheek, and he
felt the wetness between them.

"What are you thinking about, Slocum?" she asked.

Letting his arms fall, he turned away. "Nothing."

"Are you sure you're a white man?"

"Why?" He was puzzled by the question, and turned to
peer at her.

"Because you don't lie very well."

Slocum smiled in spite of himself. "You're pretty sharp.
For an Indian."

"Maybe that's because I'm only half Indian."

"Which half?"

"The half you haven't seen. The half you won't see for
a long time, if ever."

"The half I have seen, I like pretty well."

"*Now* you're talking like a white man." She shook her
head as if to say she didn't know what to do with someone
so incorrigible. "I think we better go," she said.

Without waiting for an answer, she lit out. Slocum

checked the sky, but it was no help. The stars were completely obscured. The overcast was so oppressive, he felt as if he could reach up and poke a hole in it with his finger. He was at Blue Lake's mercy. Somehow, he had the feeling it wasn't such a bad place to be—for a white man who couldn't lie very well.

She set a quick pace, her long legs easily covering the undulating ground in strides that would challenge a taller man than Slocum. In spite of his determination to keep up with her, he found himself slowly falling behind. When they had covered another two miles, she stopped for a moment. He covered the fifty-yard gap with a desperate burst, and nearly doubled over with the effort. He felt as if he were about to throw up.

He fell to the ground and lay back on the grass. His stomach felt like a gigantic knot he'd never be able to untangle. Breathing deeply, he gasped, "I guess I'm too used to horses."

She sat beside him, making sure she was out of easy reach. "No, you're just not used to not having horses. We can rest a few minutes, but we'll have to get as far as we can before sunrise."

"From the looks of that sky, there won't *be* a sunrise."

"There's snow on the way. It's early, but it happens."

"Let's hope it holds off until we get where we're going." He was breathing a little more easily now, but still panting. Talking was sapping his breath. "Is there anyplace we can get help?"

"What kind of help? Who would help us?"

"What about the Army? Is there a fort near here?"

Blue Lake laughed bitterly. "The Army? You must be joking. You don't seriously believe the Army cares about a few dead Blackfoot Indians, however they died?"

"I suppose not," he said. "What about other Indians?"

"Maybe. But they are two or three days' travel on foot. By the time we reached them, your Amanda will be long gone."

"I guess it's up to us, then," he said.

"We'd better go," she said. Blue Lake got to her feet. She reached down to take his hand and help him up. When he was on his feet, she took the carbine from him. "Maybe this will help a little." She turned and moved off. She was moving so swiftly it was as if they'd never stopped at all.

Slocum knew they were following the creek that ran past the ruined camp. He had no idea how far they had to go. And he had no idea whether he could make it. But if he was going to free Amanda, he knew he had to.

Keeping just outside the tree line, to allow maximum speed, they loped through the tall grass. From time to time a startled bird fluttered in the trees, rising with a squawk and then settling back with a few tentative chirps as they swept past. The only other sound was the whisk of their feet in the grass. That and the buzzsaw rasping of Slocum's breath in his throat, the rattle in his chest.

There was a benefit to keeping to the streambed. It was not the most direct route, but it was the levelest. The stream wound among the rolling hills, taking the easiest path. Slocum was thankful Blue Lake had not struck out across the hills. His legs felt like they were made of stone. He was long past the point where his knees throbbed. Now he couldn't feel anything below the searing pain in his thighs.

He kept moving as much because he was afraid he would never get up if he stopped again to rest as because of the urgency he felt. His body was on the verge of betraying him. Like an angry jailer, he lashed at himself, urging himself forward, daring himself to do something his tortured limbs told him he couldn't do.

Now and then he stumbled, and he allowed his momentum to carry him forward, maintaining his balance as best he could. Once it was gone, it would never be restored. An owl darted into the sky, black against the heavy gray. Slocum looked up as it swooped past. It plummeted into the grass, but its prey eluded it. The bird fluttered its thick wings and rose with an effortlessness Slocum envied. Swooping past him again, it vanished into the trees. Long after they had passed the spot, he could hear its angry hoot. It sounded as if the bird were mocking him.

His vision was starting to blur, and he felt cold. The wind was beginning to pick up, and it hissed through the leaves to his right. A few drops of cold rain splattered his cheeks. He stuck out his tongue to collect a few as they dribbled down his face.

Blue Lake was just a shadow ahead of him now. In the darkness, he could just make out her lighter shape against the thick blackness of the trees where the creek ahead curved to the left. She reached the edge of the curve, then swept to the right and vanished behind the tree line.

Slocum stumbled on, desperate to keep up. He skirted closer to the tree line to shorten the distance. He stumbled again, and this time ran into something hard, possibly a tree limb. It caught him just below the throat, stopping him cold and sending him tumbling backward into the grass. He started to rise when something in the darkness moved. He felt the foot on his heaving chest at the same moment he heard the cocking of a pistol. And he knew it wasn't a limb that had knocked him down.

Slocum stared up at the phantom in buckskin. He held up one hand as if to protect himself from the bullet he was certain was coming.

Then he heard the voice, sounding as if it came from a great distance. "Slocum . . . where are you?"

The phantom gave a start. Then, in a tongue Slocum had heard for the first time the day before, it called out.

Blue Lake answered in the same language.

"You are one lucky white man," the phantom said.

"I wish I *felt* lucky," Slocum said.

14

"I can make it on foot," Blue Lake said.

"Are you sure?" Slocum sounded doubtful. He looked at her brother, hoping to have him intercede, but he was disappointed.

"Two Bears said there were horses there," Blue Lake insisted. "From there I can go to Twin Trees to tell your friend what has happened. I can take care of myself, you both know that. Or you should."

She looked at Slocum, daring him to argue with the set of her jaw. He nodded slightly, still not convinced that Blue Lake shouldn't take one of the horses Two Bears had with him.

"Look, if I take the horse, one of you will have to go on foot. It's going to be hard enough as it is. You don't need to be making it even more difficult. Speed is important. Please, you are wasting time. Take the horses and go after them."

Two Bears stood to one side, taking no part in the discussion. He seemed faintly amused at his sister's disagreement with the white man.

Blue Lake walked toward Slocum slowly, a menacing look on her face. When she stood in front of him, she planted herself and leaned on tiptoe into his face. "Do it, I insist." She planted a kiss, half mockingly and half genuine, on his startled lips. "You know, I owe you something.

108

The sooner you leave, the sooner you can return. When you do, I can honor my obligation. I won't be free until then. Do it for me, if not for yourself. And for Amanda."

Reluctantly, Slocum nodded. "Okay," he said. "Okay. But please be careful. And make sure you tell Mrs. Dawson as little as possible. I don't want her to be any more upset than necessary. And whatever you do, don't tell her what Lavalle plans to do with Amanda."

"Don't worry," Blue Lake said. "I know how delicate white women are. Fortunately, I am only half as delicate."

"Shut up," Two Bears snapped. "You talk too much."

She whirled on her brother, her chin thrust defiantly toward him. "What I say, and to whom, is my business. Besides, he already knows."

"One of these days you are going to say too much."

"And what of it? It will be my problem, not yours. So don't trouble yourself about it."

"I guess we better go," Slocum said. He was trying to defuse an apparently explosive situation. Blue Lake was right, they were already late. If they were to have any chance at all of catching up to Clyde Lavalle, they had to get moving.

The thick gray overhead was beginning to brighten as Blue Lake stepped into the trees and disappeared. Slocum cocked his head after her, but not a sound came back to him except the gurgle of the creek. He looked at Two Bears, who stared back impassively.

"I guess we better go," Slocum said.

Two Bears nodded. In the semidarkness, it was impossible to get a good look at the Indian. All Slocum knew was that Two Bears was an inch or two taller than he was, and packed a hell of a wallop.

Slocum swung up onto the second horse. He wasn't used to riding Indian style, but he couldn't worry about such trivial matters as a saddle. Not now. The Indian kicked his horse, and the animal jumped into full gallop almost immediately. Slocum squeezed his knees against his own horse, gripping the rib cage and hanging on for dear life. He kicked it, and it spurted forward, nearly tossing Slocum to the ground.

It was too dark to be certain, but he thought he caught a glimpse of Two Bears looking back and laughing. But pride had no place in his life, not now, now when so much was at stake. Slocum was determined not to embarrass himself if at all possible, but if he had to sacrifice a little self-esteem in order to get the job done, then so be it.

The sky continued to brighten, the dark gray slowly whitening like paint on a palette as the wind stirred it and patiently mixed the sun in. Streaks of fiery white and bands of gray-black swept across the sky. As dawn approached, Slocum could see Two Bears up ahead of him. The Indian had settled into a steady rhythm, making as much time as he could without leaving Slocum hopelessly behind.

Slocum felt as if he were somehow hampering Two Bears, but for the moment there was nothing he could do. He wondered whether the Indian would be brave enough, or foolish enough, to take on Lavalle and his men single-handed. It seemed as if that had been his intention, since he had no way of knowing his sister was still alive. Following the trail of the wagons, he had stumbled on Slocum and his sister purely by chance.

Even from a distance, the Indian resembled a spring wound tight. His broad shoulders were knotted with taut muscle. His arms were tensed like those of a fighter with fists clenched. Slocum wondered whether the Indian's knuckles were squeezed white around the reins. There was an intensity in the man that seemed to go beyond the desire to avenge himself on those responsible for the slaughter of his friends and family and the destruction of their homes.

Slocum's knees were beginning to stiffen. Holding tight

to the galloping Indian pony was beginning to give him cramps. He thought about signaling to Two Bears, who occasionally glanced over his shoulder to make sure Slocum was keeping up, but he couldn't bring himself to do it. Sooner or later, he knew, the Indian would want to talk things over, get a little more information about Lavalle than he currently had, perhaps even plan some strategy. Slocum was determined to hang on at least that long.

The sun was well above the horizon now, but the morning brightness had begun to dim. The clouds overhead were thickening, and the air was cold. Twice, they had ridden through rain squalls, and the second one had been laced with a few clumps of wet snowflakes. Slocum didn't know whether to be thankful or worried at the possibility of snow. It would certainly hamper the wagons and, if it came down heavily enough, might even require them to stop for several hours. On the other hand, it would make his own task more difficult. Any hope of sneaking close to Lavalle's caravan, whether for simple reconnaissance or for an assault, would depend on the element of surprise.

It was true that Two Bears had the skills to creep close on his own, but that only addressed the second half of the equation. Two Bears couldn't hope to carry out an attack by himself, at least not one that had a reasonable chance of success.

And at the back of Slocum's mind was the irrevocable fact that Lavalle had a trump card. As long as Amanda Dawson was Lavalle's prisoner, one of Slocum's hands was tied. If he managed to get Lavalle backed into a tight enough corner, he might convince Lavalle to surrender the girl in exchange for escape. That was a long shot, but at least a shot. On the other side, though, was Two Bears. He was bent on revenge, and he neither knew Amanda nor had any reason to care about her or her safety. If getting the girl back meant letting Lavalle go free, Two Bears was almost certain to balk.

Looked at from any angle, it was a bad situation. But Slocum had long since gotten used to playing the hand he'd been dealt. No more than Two Bears could he do it alone. But with so volatile and unsympathetic an ally, he relinquished considerable control and a number of options. He kept thinking of Lavalle's fascination with strategy and tactics, and wondered what the big man with the beard would do if their situations were reversed.

Trying to be objective was getting him nowhere fast. Slocum tried to occupy his mind with other matters, but he kept coming back to the problem under his nose. They had been riding for nearly three hours when Two Bears pulled up. He was nearly a quarter of a mile ahead of Slocum, who sighed with relief as he covered the distance between him and the big Indian.

Two Bears jumped down from his horse as Slocum arrived. "We should eat now," he said.

Slocum searched his face for some sign of friendliness or hospitality, but there was none. The Indian might as well have been carved from mahogany.

Squatting on his haunches, he opened a buckskin bag and pulled out a handful of dried meat in ropy strips. He set the bag on the ground and placed the meat on top of it. He ripped at one piece with his teeth, and nodded toward the rest. "Take some," he said, speaking around the jerky as he gnawed away at it.

Slocum slipped from his horse. The impact of heels on the ground sent stabbing pain through both knees. He winced, and Two Bears laughed. "Takes a long time to learn to ride like an Indian." He grinned without warmth. "Maybe forever. I never met a white man who could."

"What about you?" Slocum asked. "You're half white, aren't you? Like your sister?"

Two Bears laughed. "Half white? There's no such thing. If you're part Indian, you're all Indian, at least to the white man."

"And what about the Indians themselves?"

"What about them?"

"How tolerant are they?"

Two Bears, leaving the jerky dangling from his teeth, swept his palms out wide, one on either side. "What do you think?"

"I think the Indians can be as intolerant, as unaccepting as the white man. Neither side much cares for the other. Isn't that right?" As Slocum spoke, he found himself thinking of another set of racial problems. The skin colors were different, but the social situations might as well have been identical.

Two Bears realized what he was thinking. "I can tell by your accent that you are no stranger to questions of race mixing," he said. "I imagine you don't need me to explain the similarities."

"But, obviously, not all white men are as intolerant as the worst of us."

"Why obviously? It's not so obvious to me."

"You are living proof, and so is your sister, that that is not true."

"Oh, really?"

"She told me about your father. He must have been tolerant."

"My father was a great man. But the fact that he had a white skin did not make him a white man. And the way his family and friends treated my mother . . ."

"But . . ."

"No buts, damn it! You think because I speak English well you can talk to me like a white man, but you can't. White education doesn't make me a white man. I'm not white, and you are. My father was a trapper who was trapped by his own skin. He thought like an Indian, admired the Indians, and was lucky enough, when necessity drove him to it, to be accepted by the Indians as one of their own. They *made* him an Indian. And that's just fine with me."

"Look, Two Bears, I—"

"And I better not find out you've laid so much as a single finger on my sister. She doesn't think like a white woman, but you think like a white man. Sex is different for us. It means something different. Hell, it *is* different. It's meaningful. You treat my sister like a whore, and so help me, I'll cut your goddamned heart out and feed it to the dogs. You understand me?"

"What your sister and I may or may not have done, or may or may not do, is a matter between the two of us. No more and no less. Do *you* understand *me*?"

Both men lapsed into silence. Slocum was determined that he would not be the first to break it. If he had a prayer of exercising any control over the events of the next few days, he had to assert himself as an equal. Right here and right now, he thought.

Slocum snatched a piece of the dried meat and began to chew it. It was tough, and oversalty, but he was hungry and it would have to do. He chewed the meat until his jaws ached, taking three pieces in all, then walked down to the creek to wash away the salty taste. He drank deeply, repeatedly sticking his face into the fast-moving water. It was so cold it nearly numbed his teeth, but he swallowed mouthful after mouthful. When he had slaked his thirst, he splashed cold water on his face and let it run down his neck.

When he got to his feet, Two Bears was standing just inside the trees. He watched Slocum shake himself free of the water. With folded arms, he leaned against a tree, his face still motionless. When Slocum walked toward him, he pushed himself away from the tree, using his upper arm. He looked at Slocum for a long moment, as if he were debating whether or not to apologize or continue the argument. In the end, he did neither. He extended his hand, and Slocum took it in his own.

Silently, Two Bears turned and walked back to the horses. He waited for Slocum to mount up, then urged his pony ahead. He was still making good time, but this time, Slocum thought, it was urgency that drove the Indian, not a desire to show up the white man trailing forlornly behind him.

It wasn't friendship, but it was a start.

15

Night fell almost without notice. The unrelieved gray of the afternoon had been mixed with swirls of rain and flurries of wet snow. By dusk, they were used to the dreary sky. When the invisible sun finally slipped away, neither Slocum nor Two Bears wanted to stop, but they were forced to rest the horses.

Over the evening meal, a replay of the morning, neither man spoke. Each was wrapped in his own thoughts, each with his own purpose. Slocum was conscious of a shift in Two Bears' attitude toward him. The silence no longer grated on his nerves. The undercurrent of hostility that had hummed in the background like a distant buzzsaw was finally quiet. Slocum had won the Indian's respect. He was more at ease on the Indian pony now, and, although no match for Two Bears, he sensed that in the Indian's eyes he was a credit to his race.

While they ate, the wind, which had been intermittent, began to blow more steadily. It moaned in the trees, and the swaying trees began to bend before the stiff assault, their heavy branches creaking in protest. Some of the closely spaced cottonwoods began to knock into one another, the dull and hollow impacts carried away on the wind.

Slocum watched the sky with apprehension. Neither man was dressed for winter, and if the storm didn't hold

off, they could be in big trouble. Conscious of Two Bears'
naked chest, Slocum sloughed off his vest and offered it to
the Indian. To Slocum's surprise, it was accepted.

Finishing their meal, they prepared to mount up. Two
Bears slipped into the trees to relieve himself and came
back with an embarrassed grin. Slocum grinned back. It
was the first genuine good feeling they had permitted
themselves.

The horses were dead tired. They had been pushed almost to the limit of their endurance. Slocum knew they
were getting close to Lavalle, but they couldn't afford to
kill their horses in the chase.

Slocum was surprised the caravan had managed to cover
as much ground as it had. He was beginning to wonder
whether Lavalle might not have struck out across the hills,
taking a more direct route at the expense of the ease afforded by the flatland along the creek bed. He thought
about raising the question with Two Bears, but he didn't
want to offend him.

The Indian sensed that something was bothering his
companion. "What is it?"

"I was just thinking," Slocum answered. "Lavalle seems
to have gotten pretty far. I know Blue Lake and I hadn't
covered that much ground. I would have thought we would
have caught up to him by now."

"We would have, if that's what we were trying to do."

"What *are* we trying to do, then?"

"Skin two rabbits with one knife."

Slocum was confused.

Two Bears explained. "We need winter clothes, and we
want to get ahead of them. They will assume they are
being followed. Since you and my sister escaped, it is the
only logical thing for them to do. They will be watching
their tails. But they won't expect us to be ahead of them.

We are taking the long way around, but we are moving faster than they can."

"That assumes you know where they are headed."

"A man has to take a chance now and then. It is logical that they would follow the wagon route. They have to realize that it will be snowing before morning. They may not know that it will be heavy, but they won't stray too far from the established route. It is the safest thing for them to do."

"I hope you're right," Slocum said.

"So do I," Two Bears answered. "If not, we may never find them again."

Slocum climbed onto the pony with a sigh. His knees still ached. He could ignore the pain while riding, but every time he rested, they began to swell.

Two Bears noticed the gritted teeth and the flash of pain on Slocum's face. "We can do something about that, too. If you wore lighter footwear, your knees wouldn't have to work so hard. You are straining to keep those heavy boots in the air."

The Indian sounded like it really mattered, and Slocum was grateful. "Thanks," he said. "But I'm going to find Lavalle if I have to go barefoot in the snow to do it."

"Let's hope it won't come to that."

Slocum nodded his agreement.

As if summoned by his words, a sudden flurry of snow swirled down out of the trees. The wind howled briefly, and the snow thickened in the air. For the first time, flakes failed to melt on contact with the ground.

Two Bears climbed onto his pony. "We better hurry," he said.

The snow picked up, and the wind suddenly died away. The only sound was the distant gurgle of the creek and the steady hiss of the icy flakes sifting through the trees and the stiff grass. They gray air was full of swirling clots of snow. Their visibility, already diminished by the absence of sun, was further reduced.

The horses seemed frightened by the weather. Slocum's pony kept tossing its head, as if trying to turn around. He kept a tight rein on the animal, pushing it as fast as he dared in the short visibility. It was beginning to snow harder now, and the flakes were no longer wet. They stung his cheeks like icy bees, slashing across his face at an angle despite the absence of wind.

Two Bears had moderated his pace, as much out of concern for the ponies' footing as for Slocum. The snow had begun to collect on the horses' manes, and Slocum's hat felt heavy as the accumulated snow weighed down its brim.

They were heading slowly higher as the ground rose toward the western mountains. The ascent was steeper than it had been, although still gentle. They hit a rise, and Two Bears took his horse up at an angle, easing away from the creek and picking his way carefully through the stony rubble.

As they reached the top of the rise, Two Bears came to a sudden halt. Slocum pulled up beside him. He was about to ask why they had stopped when the snowy veils shifted slightly and he was able to answer his own question. In the valley below them a thin yellowish cloud had appeared for a few seconds before the snow swirled back and swept it away.

"What is that light?" Slocum asked.

"It is the camp of my friend Lone Calf," Two Bears told him. "But I don't understand why there is so much light. There are only four families in the village. And they wouldn't have a fire going in the open in this weather." His voice sounded like a humming wire. The tension was unmistakable. Two Bears eased his pony over the top of the rise and started to angle down along the snowy slope. He descended carefully, zigzagging across the face of the rise in a series of switchbacks, even though there was no trail. The normally surefooted ponies were having increasing difficulty on the snow-slickened grass. The snow melted under their hooves, and the grass became like an oiled slide beneath them.

The descent was agonizingly slow. Twice Slocum's pony slipped and nearly fell. Two Bears, comfortable with the style of riding, had less trouble, but even he was extraordinarily cautious. When they hit the floor of the valley, the Indian clucked to his pony, flapping his legs against its ribs to urge it forward. Slocum tried to keep up, but the urgency in Two Bears' voice had been translated into breakneck speed on the treacherous footing.

The Indian had all but disappeared, reduced to an occasional blob of shadow between Slocum and the source of the yellow light. It was difficult to gauge the distance, but Slocum guessed he still had a quarter mile to go when he heard a howl that made his heart stop for a long moment. The sound was inhuman, starting as a low pitched growl and culminating in a piercing shriek that seemed to stab Slocum in the chest. He had no doubt the author of the sound was Two Bears, but he couldn't imagine what could have provoked such a terrifying sound.

Slocum pushed his pony to move even faster as the sound was repeated, then slowly died in a shuddering crescendo. He plunged ahead, watching the yellow blur slowly sharpen. The swirling snow lifted for a few seconds, and Slocum saw Two Bears, now no longer on horseback, starkly outlined against the glow.

When he dismounted, he rushed forward, his feet slipping on the snowy grass. He heard the crackle of flames before he could see what was burning. And when he finally drew close enough to see clearly through the freezing curtain he stopped in his tracks. There, in miniature, was a recreation of the carnage of Two Bears' own village. One tepee was blazing, having been doused with something flammable. The others were intact, although charred, as if the flames had tried to consume them and failed.

And the haphazard array of bodies, too, was gruesomely familiar. Two Bears had fallen to his knees. He rocked back and forth, his head cradled in his hands. The first howl of grief had died away. In its place, was an icy silence disturbed only by the wind and the crackle of the flames.

Slocum walked to the big Indian and knelt beside him. "We'll get even," he said.

Two Bears shook his head slowly. "But first we have to take care of the dead."

"I'll give you a hand."

"No!" Two Bears turned on him in a fury. "I'll do it myself. Your kind has already done enough." He rose to his feet and walked into the center of the small camp. He knelt again, this time beside the body of an old man. He bent low, as if to whisper in the old man's ear. Slocum realized it must be the body of Lone Calf. Then, cradling the ancient head in his hands, Two Bears looked up at the sky. It was the oldest scene in history, a man looking to the heavens, daring it to explain the unexplainable, to defend the indefensible.

Slocum, too, looked up. He saw nothing but swirling snow against an impregnable gray sky.

16

By morning the snow had stopped. The sun came out slowly, poking through the clouds as if trying to make up its mind whether to stay. The white shroud did nothing to conceal the wreckage of Lone Calf's small encampment. Three of the four tepees were charred shells, their skin walls burned away to nothing. The poles, charred through in many places, looked frail, like the skeletons of old women. The one tepee still relatively intact looked out of place among the ruins.

Two Bears stepped into the sunlight with several pieces of clothing draped over one arm. In the other, he held a bow and quiver. In the new age, the weapons were every bit as much remnants of a dead era as the ruined dwellings and the dead bodies lying in the snow.

Slocum watched the Indian as he walked around the camp one more time. Idly kicking at clumps of snow, as if searching for something, maybe a reason it all had happened, Two Bears seemed wrapped in an impregnable, personal gloom. When he had satisfied himself that he would not find whatever it was he was looking for, he walked over to Slocum and sat on the ground. Despite the cold, he ignored the snow.

Sorting through the clothing, he handed Slocum a jacket lined with rabbit skins. He also gave back the vest Slocum had lent him. Slowly he stood up and slipped into a buckskin shirt and covered it with a jacket similar to the one he had given Slocum.

"What do you want to do about the bodies?" Slocum asked. Two Bears started as if he had been unaware of Slocum's presence. He seemed to consider the question for a long moment, then shook his head without saying anything. After a long pause, he turned to the white man. The look in his eyes was distant and nearly impenetrable, like the deepest well Slocum had ever seen. And at its bottom was a spark of unmistakable rage. For a few seconds his lips trembled soundlessly. When he finally spoke, it was in a hoarse whisper. "There is no time."

"I understand," Slocum said.

"No, you don't understand. You can't understand. I feel as if I am pursued by a part of myself. It is as if that part of me I try to hide, just as my father tried to hide the same thing in himself, keeps haunting me."

"You mean the white part, don't you?"

Two Bears didn't answer. He didn't have to.

In silence, the two men prepared to break camp. Each man seemed immersed in his own thoughts, and neither was willing to disrupt the concentration of the other.

Slocum was preoccupied with the carnage he had seen in the last two days. Clyde Lavalle had seemed like a rational man, even an intelligent one. He spoke with feeling about those things that mattered to him. But while the man's intelligence was unquestionable, his sanity was another matter.

It wasn't rational to destroy people who simply said no, they weren't interested in what you happened to be selling. And it wasn't rational to abduct two young women to sell them into prostitution. It might make some perverse kind of commercial sense, but Lavalle seemed to be an example of the entrepreneurial spirit run amok. His credo seemed to be, "Anything for a buck. And fuck you if you're not in the market."

But if Lavalle was deranged, his intelligence made him even more dangerous. Finding him might not be so difficult—at least not for a man with Two Bears' skills or Slocum's determination. But catching him would be harder to do. Slocum knew he would have to proceed carefully. And he also knew that the hatred slowly simmering over the hot flame of Two Bears' rage made for a combustible commodity. In a way, Slocum was trapped between two explosive, unpredictably volatile men. Getting away without getting blown to pieces wasn't going to be easy. And getting Amanda Dawson back unharmed looked to be damned near impossible.

The sun began to work its magic on the snow as they mounted up. Two inches of fluff had begun to turn into translucent soup. The green of the grass beneath the melting snow looked like the leaves of water plants. Slocum half expected to see small fish darting in among them, frightened by the unexpected hooves of the horses. Despite the sun, it was still cold. As the morning wore on, Slocum kept glancing at the sky. Something in the air told him they had not seen the last of the snow.

He goosed the pony and eased up alongside Two Bears, who was watching the ground. "Looks like we're in for more snow in a few hours," he said.

"We are. And we won't get off so easily this time." Two Bears looked at him sideways, a half smile on his lips. It seemed to Slocum that the snow wasn't the only thing thawing under the bright sunlight.

The noise of their ponies sounded like a small cavalry patrol as they sloshed through the soupy slush.

To Slocum there were no visible signs of Lavalle's passage. As far as he could tell, he and Two Bears were the first men in a thousand years to pass this way. But the

Indian was intent on something. As the snow melted, it became easier, and he quickened his pace. Slocum wanted to ask what Two Bears was looking for, but he already felt inadequate. The Indian would hardly pass up the opportunity to remind him just how far out of his element he truly was. As if he needed any such reminder.

The sun finally broke through altogether, the last remnant of misty clouds disappearing like smoke in a stiff wind. The air still carried the promise of more snow. It smelled damp, despite the cold.

By noon, traces of white on the grass were few and far between. Occasionally, in a hollow in the ground where more had collected, and in the shadows of rocks and trees, where the sun couldn't get at it, a few clumps remained. They were so bright in the unchallenged sun that they hurt the eyes. They lay like rags, the ruins of a bridal party, their contours shaped more by happenstance than by any orderly hand, visible or invisible.

The land beneath them rose at a sharper angle now. The mountains were still far to the west, at least a day's ride away. But there was no mistaking the steady rise. The horses began to labor a little, their breathing coming faster to compensate for the thinning air. Slocum noticed his own breathing adjusting to the increased altitude. Beyond the mountains, huge clouds piled up as the wet air climbed past the jagged peaks.

By two o'clock, Slocum was ravenous. "We have to stop for a while," he called to the big Indian.

Two Bears made a face, but he jerked his pony to a halt. "Twenty minutes, no more. We're getting close now. I don't want them to slip away again."

"How far?"

"Not sure. They're about three hours ahead of us, but we're moving faster than they are. It won't take us that long to catch up. But it will be near nightfall."

"That's all right," Slocum said. "We can do a little reconnaissance, see what we're up against. It wouldn't hurt to have some sort of plan. I'm not crazy about the direct approach. Not in this case."

"They're only men," Two Bears reminded him.

"But Lavalle is no ordinary man. That much I'm certain about."

"Even extraordinary men bleed if you cut them deeply enough. It is wise to respect your enemy, but it is foolish to respect him too much."

"Is that some old Blackfoot wisdom?" Slocum said, smiling.

"Actually, no. It was Ulysses S. Grant. One of yours, I believe."

"Not quite," Slocum said. "Right war, wrong side."

Two Bears just grunted.

Slocum was already tired of subsisting on dried meat. He groaned when Two Bears handed him three of the chewy strips. "What is this stuff, anyway? It has a gamy taste. Kind of strong."

"It's good for you."

"Don't talk like my mother. Everything you hate is good for you."

"My mother did it to me," Two Bears laughed. "I'm just carrying on an honorable tradition."

"You're not going to tell me what it is, are you?" Slocum held the meat at a distance and eyed it suspiciously. "It's so damned stringy."

"It'll keep you alive, that's all you need to know."

Slocum frowned, but he knew the Indian was right. He resumed his chomping, tugging at the ropy strips with his incisors, trying to rip small pieces away for easier chewing.

As he chewed, it dawned on him that Two Bears' mother was one of Lavalle's victims. The big Indian seemed to remember at the same instant. His face clouded over.

Slocum tried to change the subject. "How long before the snow?"

Two Bears jerked as if he'd been struck. He looked at Slocum for a long moment without speaking. Finally he raised his head to sniff the air. He glanced at the sky as if to confirm the information his nostrils had gathered. "Not long."

The wind shifted suddenly, and Two Bears got to his feet. He wiped his hands on the buckskin jacket, leaving shiny smears where the greasy meat had stained his fingers. He looked at the soft leather as if he had never seen it before, then pulled up a handful of damp grass and wiped at the grease. The water darkened the leather, but the greasy smears were still visible, now refracting the sunlight into rainbow spatters.

"Let's go," he said.

Slocum stuck the remainder of the meat into his pocket, intending to finish it as they rode. He was growing fond of the volatile Indian. At first he had seemed so different from Blue Lake that it was difficult to credit their being brother and sister. But now, as the Indian seemed to be more comfortable with him, flashes of Blue Lake kept dancing into Two Bears' behavior. Both were quixotic, both given to plain speaking, and, as much as Two Bears would deny it, both had mischievous senses of humor.

They were gaining on Lavalle. Slocum felt it in his gut, and common sense would have told him the same thing. The wagons were heavily loaded. Four-horse teams were no match for a pair of fast Indian ponies, even if the wagons had been empty. And Lavalle's method was driven by commercial interest. He was looking for customers, even as he ran for the mountain passes. There was no sense of fear in the man, and, despite having committed two separate outrages against human decency, Slocum didn't believe that Lavalle was frightened. If anything, he probably welcomed the game of cat and mouse. And Slocum wasn't sure he could tell the feline from the rodent.

Not yet, anyway.

As the sun began to slide down behind the mountains, they picked up their pace, hoping to narrow the gap before nightfall, perhaps even to make visual contact. But when they reached the crest of a long, gentle ridge, they had more visual contact than they had bargained for.

Far below them, three or four miles away across the broad valley, Slocum saw Lavalle's wagons. And he saw another half dozen or so as well.

"I thought you said there were only three wagons," Two Bears said. His voice was like cold steel on a whetstone, and Slocum knew he was angry.

"That's all there were. I don't know who the others are. Or where in hell they came from. I wish I had binoculars."

Two Bears grunted. He reached into a leather bag hanging over his horse's rump. When he brought his hand back, he held a small leather tube. Slocum had seen one before. This one bore the same metal stamping on its side. The gold "U.S." marked it as Army issue. Two Bears flipped the tube to him, and Slocum eagerly unscrewed the cap. He tilted the tube and carefully removed the telescope. Its brass fittings were no longer shiny, but the leather binding showed evidence of careful attention. He popped the lens covers off and opened the scope.

"Where'd you get this?" Slocum asked.

"My sister and I found it one day, when we were playing. I was older so I got to keep it. We found other things, too, but this was easy to get to."

"Get to? I don't understand."

"The smell—dead horses and dead cavalrymen. Dead

Indians, too. The flies were ferocious, so we only walked along the edge of the battlefield."

Slocum inhaled sharply, then let his breath out in a long, slow stream. No matter which way he turned, it seemed impossible to get away from the bitterness. Not that he blamed Two Bears for his feelings; that wouldn't have been fair. But the feelings ran so deep, and were so easily triggered, he pitied the man who had to carry such poison inside him.

Slocum dropped from his horse and scooted forward on his hands and knees, taking care not to get the telescope wet. When he was at the highest point on the ridge, he brought the scope to bear on the scene below. A dozen men scurried around, lugging heavy kegs from one wagon to another. It looked as if Lavalle was restocking his own caravan.

The sun was beginning to set, and the reddish cast of the light made the valley floor look as if it were catching fire. The black figures flitting through the fiery backdrop reminded Slocum of a picture he had seen in a magazine in New Orleans—or St. Louis, he wasn't sure. The only difference was the color. The picture had been black and white, all lines and patches of shade. This was all too real. But both were scenes from hell.

In the telescope's lens, he could resolve the figures into recognizable faces. He saw Jed staggering under the weight of a keg, and Martin, standing to one side, probably complaining, as usual. Lavalle was there too, surveying the transfer like a ship's captain supervising the loading of cargo.

But one figure stood out among all the others. In frayed blue shirt and dungarees, Amanda Dawson cowered at Lavalle's knees. The glittering handcuffs on her wrists flashed like distress beacons. She couldn't know it, but someone had seen the signal for help.

Now all Slocum had to do was figure out how to answer it.

Slocum paced nervously on the wet ground. His feet had trampled the grass into green pulp. The Indian had been gone for nearly two hours. In the darkness, the scene on the valley floor was the only thing he could see, and his eyes kept coming back to it. Every fifteen minutes he lay on the ground and swept across the camp with the telescope, but the light from campfires was sporadic, and much of the area was draped in shadows.

Amanda Dawson had been hustled into one of the wagons nearly an hour before, and Slocum hadn't seen her since. He had been gratified that she appeared to be unhurt, but resolving the focus and zeroing in on her face had shown him the unmistakable terror. Her eyes had seemed glazed, but they darted incessantly, as if she felt threatened from every side.

Slocum had known that finding Lavalle was the easier part of his problem. Now that he had done that, he found himself face to face with the more difficult half, and he didn't know what to do. It was like staring at a brick wall so high you couldn't see over it, and so long there was no way around it.

He wanted Two Bears to return with some miraculous message, a detailed analysis of some unexpected chink in Lavalle's armor. But he knew that wasn't going to happen. For the moment, and for the forseeable future, it was two men against a small army. You didn't have to be a student of history to understand how long the odds were. They had justice on their side, but that seldom made a difference. Good men were routinely and regularly crushed by bad men with superior firepower. Slocum knew it, and Two Bears, despite his determination, knew it too. Neither man wanted to admit it to the other, but whether they talked about it or kept quiet, it was there.

The camp fires were beginning to burn down. The light cast by each continued to shrink. The gaps of darkness between spread like stains on a tablecloth. Slocum was on the verge of moving in for a closer look when he spotted Two Bears loping toward him up the grass-covered slope.

The Indian was out of breath from the long uphill climb. He dropped to his haunches and struggled to catch his breath. Slocum was anxious to know what he had learned, but Two Bears held up a hand to wave off any questions. Slocum handed him a canteen, and Two Bears took a long pull on the water, swallowing with audible gulps.

Tossing the canteen back to Slocum, he watched until it was recapped and tossed aside.

"What'd you find out," Slocum asked.

Two Bears swallowed hard, then coughed. "Lavalle's pulling out," he said.

"When?"

"An hour or so. As soon as he can."

"Why?"

"I'm not sure. There was some kind of argument. Lavalle was furious. They had to pull him off the leader of the other group—Murchison, the guy's name is. Something about the price of whiskey. Lavalle claims Murchison is trying to hold him up. They had agreed on a price, and now Murchison wants more. I don't think he'll get it, but it's close to open war down there. Lavalle is getting another wagon and a couple more men."

"Shit!" Slocum stood up and started to pace in tight circles.

"What's wrong, Slocum? It's better for us if they do split up."

"Yeah, maybe. But if I know Lavalle, he'll be expecting trouble. He'll have more security. We'll have a hell of a time getting close to him now. That makes things tougher.'"

"We'll manage."

"What about Murchison? What's he going to do?"

"I don't know for certain. I think he's going to stay put. There's supposed to be somebody else coming to meet him. Near as I can figure it out, Murchison is some kind of supplier to a whole bunch of teams like Lavalle's."

"A wholesaler. Jesus! I've seen everything now." Slocum was on the verge of laughing out loud. He shook his head in frustration. "Damn it!"

"I still think it could be good for us," Two Bears insisted.

"Do you think Murchison would help Lavalle if he got in trouble?"

"I don't understand what you're asking me."

"If we take Lavalle on, will Murchison throw in with him? How mad were they?"

"If I had to guess, I'd say no. They don't like each other, that much is clear. And Murchison has already been paid. It seems to me that he wouldn't care if Lavalle disappeared altogether. I don't think they can do business again. That seems to be the only thing they have in common. Take that away, neither one of them has any reason to care if the other lives or dies. In fact, I don't think either one would mind if the other *did* die."

Slocum widened his circle. His pacing slowed as he stroked his chin. "There has to be a way we can use that to our advantage."

"What do you suggest?"

"First, let's decide what we want to accomplish here. If I understand you, you'd be just as happy to take Murchison out, as well as Lavalle. Is that right?"

Two Bears nodded slowly. "Yes," he said. "But you don't care either way, is that right?"

"No, it's not right. After what I've seen in the past few

days . . ." Slocum stopped, choking back the revulsion he'd been struggling against ever since the attack on the first Blackfoot village. He swallowed hard, then tried again. "I'd be happy to put an end to the whole pack of them. Lavalle, Murchison, whoever. If Lavalle didn't have Amanda Dawson, I wouldn't mind staying here, taking out Murchison and whoever he's waiting to meet, then going after Lavalle. But I can't afford to wait."

"All right then. Suppose we split up."

"What good would that do?" Slocum asked, stopping in his tracks and facing Two Bears in the dim light.

"You can follow Lavalle, so you don't lose track of him. I'll do what I can here, and I'll catch up with you."

"You can't take on that bunch all by yourself. That's crazy."

"Yes," the Indian said, "I can. And I will. I'm not interested in killing everybody down there. But I want the leaders dead. The others don't matter to me. They won't come back. And I want the whiskey destroyed."

"I still think you're crazy. It was Lavalle that killed your people, Lavalle and his men, not Murchison."

"No, Slocum, that's where you are wrong. It wasn't Lavalle, and it wasn't whiskey. It was greed, the kind of greed that white men call business. Do whatever you have to do to make another man give you money in exchange for something he doesn't want and doesn't need. Killing Lavalle and killing Murchison, that's just an indirect step. Greed won't die with them. But it will make other greedy men think twice before coming here. Look at these hills, Slocum. There used to be buffalo by the millions here. Now you can go weeks without seeing a single one. And for what? An animal that would keep a whole family alive for half a year was shot to death for nothing, the meat left to rot in the sun. That's greed, and that's what I want to put a stop to. If it means I have to kill a few men, then I will. Because if I don't do it, if I don't take that chance, then I have no right to expect another man to do it. And it has to be done. If you are honest with yourself, you'll see that I am right."

Slocum said nothing. He was no stranger to greed. His own family had been destroyed by greedy men, his whole future taken from him, his life indelibly stained so that a few greedy men could have more of something they didn't need.

"Okay," he said.

Two Bears stood and covered the distance between them in two steps. He grasped Slocum's forearm and squeezed. "You won't be sorry. I promise you that."

Slocum turned his back to stare down into the valley. The fires had continued to contract. They were little more than heaps of embers now; what little light they threw off died within a few feet. The rest of the makeshift bivouac was a jumble of shade and shadow.

Occasionally, something impenetrable moved past one or another of the dying fires, momentarily blocking the feeble glow. It was as if the men down there were defining themselves unknowingly. The blackness, the absence of light was the only evidence of their existence. Just as the ruined village of Blue Lake and Two Bears, the small holocaust that had taken Lone Calf and his clan, were the only signs that Clyde Lavalle had passed that way.

Slocum sat on the wet grass, sweeping the valley with the telescope. It was difficult to see anything, even with its assistance. In his anxiety, he tapped the slender tube of the telescope with his fingers. Finally, a wagon lurched out of the firelight.

It was time to go.

17

Two Bears slipped along inside the edge of the tree line, keeping a wary eye on the nervous sentry. The man kept looking into the trees. At each sound, he shifted his position, swiveling his head in response to every natural noise. The wagons were silent, the rest of the men having gone to sleep.

The guard was twenty yards in front of Two Bears, his back protected by a small stand of birches. The closely packed, narrow trunks arched away on both sides, enclosing the sentry in a shallow bowl. Two Bears would not be able to slip among the birches without alerting the guard. As yet, he had no idea how he would get close enough to dispose of the man. He would have to rely on luck, but first he would have to get close enough for luck to be of some use.

When he was ten yards away, he could just make out the head and shoulders of the guard. The head was still twisting this way and that in response to the slightest sound. A katydid twisted it one way, a locust another. When a frog bellowed then dove into the shallow water of the creek, the guard almost lost control. It would have been funny in other circumstances, but Two Bears saw nothing amusing in the situation.

So far, all the sentry had done was look. Nothing he had heard was of sufficient interest to move the man out of his cover, which arched over his back like the shell of a turtle. The man seemed to be on the edge of nervous collapse, and Two Bears wondered how to get him out of the cover without sending him running to the wagons or firing blindly into the trees. If the rest of the camp was awakened, Two Bears would be able to do nothing.

The Indian was no more than fifteen feet away now, but it might as well have been fifteen miles. Using a gun was out of the question, and Two Bears couldn't get close enough to use a knife. Somehow, he would have to lure the guard out of his protective shell. The ground was littered with small twigs and strips of dry bark. Reaching down, Two Bears grabbed a handful of the dead wood and bark. He took a twig and flipped it off to one side. It landed soundlessly, and Two Bears clenched his jaw in frustration. He tried again, this time with a larger twig.

The sentry turned his head abruptly as the twig clacked against a tree limb before landing in the grass. He stared into the darkness, his face frozen. He held his breath and leaned toward the sound, as if the few inches would make a difference.

The guard shifted his feet, and Two Bears tensed. There might be just one chance, and he had to be ready for it. The guard took a tentative step toward the fallen twig, cocking his head from side to side, then back, like a bird. In his head, Two Bears was shouting at the man to move. In desperation, he tossed another twig, flipping it with his wrist to keep motion to a minimum. The twig clacked against something hard, possibly a stone, and the guard took two more steps.

Two Bears shifted his position, placing his feet carefully and backing slightly away from the trees to make sure his clothing didn't scrape against the rough bark. The guard moved again, taking a longer step this time. As he moved, he shifted his rifle nervously from hand to hand. He still hadn't chambered a round, and Two Bears was certain he wouldn't have been foolish enough to have kept it live without reason.

Two Bears could now see his prey from the waist up. They were dancing around a maypole, the guard moving one way and Two Bears a semicircle behind. Two Bears prayed for luck to intervene. Another frog croaked, in the trees beyond the guard, then leapt into the water, landing with a splash that moved the sentry three more steps.

Two Bears now had a clean shot at the guard. He slipped a knife from its sheath at his waist and brought it up chest high, ready to dive at the sentry if he began to turn. Two Bears took a long step, then froze as the sentry worked the lever on his Winchester. The sound of the cartridge slamming home sounded deafening in the quiet.

Daring another stride, Two Bears shifted the knife to his left hand. Six feet in front of him, the guard had all but turned to stone. Two Bears could see his shoulders moving slightly with the shallow breaths of a terrified man. The raspy breathing sawed at the silence, and Two Bears tensed himself, waiting for the inevitable shriek as it finally gave way.

Another step, and he was close enough. Steeling himself, the big Indian coiled like a spring, releasing the tension almost immediately. He slammed into the guard, who was nearly as tall, but not nearly as bulky as the Indian. Snaking his right arm around the sentry's neck, he clamped it tightly under the chin, squeezing the larynx and crushing the first cry to gurgling pulp in the guard's throat.

The Winchester thumped to the ground as the sentry reached for the forearm cutting off his air. He dug his nails into the buckskin sleeve, but the leather protected Two Bears' skin and the Indian leaned backward, hauling the sentry first to tiptoe, then off the ground altogether. He felt the guard's heels slamming into his shins. The man twisted and turned like a fish on a line, and Two Bears feared he might lose his grip. The sentry was young, and for a moment, the Indian felt a twinge of conscience. As he remembered the burning ruins of his village, the twinge passed. He slid the knife across the collarbone, using his leathered forearm as a straightedge. The sudden bubbling told him he'd severed the windpipe. The struggle weakened almost at once.

And then the heels stopped cracking into his shins. When he let the guard go, he dropped like a gutted deer. Two Bears bent to wipe his blade clean in the tall grass, then slipped it back into its sheath. He stood for a moment, looking down at the dead man. He thought he might regret it. But he felt nothing.

The wagons were light gray hulks against the darker gray of the overcast sky. The next step would be to prepare them for destruction. Arranged in a loose ring, their horses in a makeshift corral, they had to be entered one by one. Two Bears stepped to the nearest wagon and peered into the ring. More than a dozen men lay sleeping. Their bedrolls were rumpled, and two or three of the men tossed and turned. Nerves on edge, they were barely asleep.

Using his knife, Two Bears cut the laces on the first canvas cover and hauled himself silently into the wagon. The interior was too dark for an inventory. He groped with his hands until he found the familiar shape of a whiskey keg. Stacks of the kegs, standing upright, were lashed into the front end of the wagon.

Targeting the upper row, Two Bears felt along the contours of the kegs until he found what he was looking for. Prying the bunghole plug out of the rock-hard oak took several minutes. When he had it almost free, he stepped back away from the kegs and leaned forward on his toes to pop it loose. The sudden burbling of the escaping liquid sounded like a torrent in the close confines.

The whiskey splashed over the kegs below it, and splattered his clothes. Inside the canvas, the smell was overwhelming. Easing back to the ground, he closed the canvas again, tugging the ends tight but unable to lace them shut. He peeked into the circle of sleeping men. The same three still rolled. The glowing embers of the campfire shifted uneasily in a slight breeze. While he watched, a burning knot popped, scattering sparks in a broad arc, like a rainbow of a single color.

Moving swiftly outside the ring of wagons, he made his way to the next. This held only a few kegs, being devoted to carrying supplies. Sacks of flour and beans covered the floor. A few kegs were lodged against the front end of the wagon, and he opened one, then lifted it to sprinkle the volatile whiskey over the sacks. He slit one of the sacks and emptied its contents on the floor of the wagon, draping the cloth over his shoulder.

In quick succession, he entered the remaining wagons. In all but one case, he had found at least one keg of whiskey. The sole exception was full of ammunition and kegs of black powder. Running whiskey was not without risks, and Murchison had come more than adequately prepared to defend himself and his caravan.

The remaining work was critical. Two Bears knew that his timing had to be perfect if he were to have a chance of success. He couldn't torch the wagons until he got rid of the horses. But as soon as he stampeded the animals, the camp would explode into life. The men were heavily armed, and he had to assume they knew how to use their weapons. He lugged two small kegs with him, groaning under their weight.

Moving to the corral, he sat down on its far side. The horses muttered among themselves, and he backed off a bit, staying still until they got used to his presence. As soon as they quieted down, he went to work. He prepared several arrows, wrapping each in a strip of the sackcloth, knotting the material just above the arrowheads.

Opening one of the kegs, he made small balls of black powder in squares of the cloth, then used strands of the tough grass to secure them to the arrows. When he had a dozen arrows prepared, he was just about ready. He opened the second keg, grain alcohol by its smell, and let each of the cloth wrappings drink its fill of the combustible fluid.

With his knife, he cut the reins by which the horses had been tethered in the makeshift triangular remuda. When all the horses were free, he cut the rope on the side away from camp then shooed the horses, trying to keep as quiet as he could. As the first horses broke free, it sounded like all hell had broken loose. The animals began to whinny, and their hooves pounded down the slope as they raced away from the wagons.

Slipping into the darkness, he watched as the first few men appeared between the wagons. It was now or never. Using flint and steel he lit the first arrow and speared the canvas top of the nearest wagon. The bright flame dimmed momentarily on impact, then seemed to recover its strength. The canvas caught fire and a moment later burned through. The packet of powder blew a fraction of a second later, igniting the accumulated fumes in the wagon. A great ball of flame rose over the wagon, painting the trees and the lowering sky with orange.

In quick succession, he drilled one wagon after another, changing his location before each shot to make sure they couldn't get a fix on his position. Stunned by the first blast, the runners had dived for cover. Now, Murchison tried to rally his men to put out the flames. But a second wagon blew, showering flaming debris over the whole camp. All the canvas covers were ablaze.

Against the garish light, Murchison scrambled backward, his bulk starkly etched in near black. Two Bears smiled grimly. Swinging his carbine around, he waited for Murchison to reappear. Darting this way and that among the wagons, the runner kept disappearing and reappearing among the burning shadows.

The ammunition wagon began to collapse in on itself. A keg of powder blew, showering the camp with pieces of the wagon. Live rounds began to fire, sending bullets in every direction, like the swords of a magician through a black box. The men scattered, fleeing the deadly ring and rushing into the surrounding trees. Murchison, his fists clenched over his head, danced furiously in the center of camp. Two Bears sighted carefully. Another keg of powder blew, but Murchison danced on.

The trigger taut under his finger, Two Bears held his bead. In the uproar, he didn't even hear his gun go off. Murchison stopped, then jerked sideways, like a puppet brought up short. His momentum carried him backward until his feet slammed into a ruptured whiskey keg. He tumbled over backward amid a shower of burning rags as yet another wagon blew. The pool of whiskey caught fire, and Murchison tried to rise, his clothes soaked in the flaming booze. Two Bears fired again, and Murchison went down for keeps.

The hot blue flame of the burning alcohol swallowed him whole.

18

Two Bears caught up with Slocum just before sunrise. The Indian refused to talk, and Slocum respected the silence. They rode side by side for the first time, Slocum noticed.

The ground rose more sharply now as the wagons neared the mountains. Slocum and Two Bears watched with impatience as Lavalle and his men headed into a narrow valley. The only thing they could do was hang on to Lavalle's tail. The sides of the valley were too steep to permit an approach. Attacking from above was out of the question. If they were going to make a move, its success would depend as much on speed and maneuverability as anything. There were at least a dozen men. Firepower was laughably unequal.

But it was Amanda Dawson's presence that made speed essential. They would have to move in and rescue the girl before Lavalle had a chance to reassert himself by threatening the girl. Once he realized Slocum was one of the attackers, Amanda would be a pawn in a game Slocum couldn't win. And Two Bears, his appetite for vengeance only sharpened by his destruction of Murchison's supply train, was already champing at the bit. It would take very little in the way of provocation to tip him into a blind frenzy.

Riding far enough behind the small wagon train to conceal their presence was torture. To be so close, and so helpless, kept both men on edge. Their conversation was scant, and what little there was resembled a duel with razors. The sky seemed to press down on them like a sheet of lead. The Indian predicted snow within a short time, and one glance at the thickening overcast had Slocum convinced.

"I've been thinking," Slocum said, risking conversation for one last time. "Our only chance is to split them up somehow. We can take them on in twos and threes."

"Great idea, Two Bears, why didn't you think of that?" The sarcasm in the Indian's response nearly brought Slocum to a full boil. He glanced at Two Bears, who continued to talk to himself in a sarcastic undertone. "What you should do, you big, dumb Injun, is ride up to the front of Mr. Lavalle's wagon. Ask him if he wouldn't mind sending his men out two at a time for you and Slocum to kill them. Then, when nobody's left, you just take the girl and burn the wagons before you leave."

"All right, all right," Slocum barked. "I didn't say I had a way to get it done. I just said it was our best chance. I guess what I meant is that if we don't get a break soon, we don't *have* a chance."

"*You* don't," Two Bears said.

"What does that mean?"

"It means that if we don't get the break you think we need, it's over. At least as far as you are concerned. But if that happens, I can do things my way. If you give up, the girl is as good as dead. We both know that. If you walk away, I'm free to do it my way."

"Without regard to the girl's safety, you mean." Slocum was getting angry. He understood what Two Bears was saying, and part of him even agreed with the Indian. But he was unwilling to concede his own helplessness. At least, not just yet. It was near nightfall, and the wagons would soon be stopping. For the moment, all he could do was hang on and keep his fingers crossed.

Slocum lapsed into silence. The wagons were nearing the far end of the narrow valley, and it would be necessary to wait until they had passed all the way through. There was too little cover available on the valley floor to risk entering while the wagons were still there.

At the mouth of the valley, Two Bears held up his left hand. He dismounted quickly and climbed a nearby tree. It wasn't all that sturdy, but the big Indian managed to get nearly fifteen feet off the ground before the tree began to creak under his weight. He crept out onto a thick limb. It gave under him a bit, dipping toward the ground as he crept away from the trunk. With one hand, he swept away a clump of yellowing leaves and stared intently.

"What is it?" Slocum whispered.

"They've stopped."

"You don't think they're going to camp for the night, do you? It's too early."

"I don't know what they're doing. Lavalle is standing alongside one of the wagons. Wait a minute."

Balancing precariously on his knees, Two Bears used both hands to open the telescope case and extend the tube to its full length. Leaning forward again, one hand sweeping the leaves aside while the other steadied the telescope, he swayed from side to side, trying to keep his balance.

In disgust, he let go of the leaves and changed position. Sitting on the sturdy branch, he wrapped one leg around the limb and brought the other up to push the leaves out of his way. Holding the telescope with two hands, he had a stabler view.

Slocum climbed off his own horse and stood right beneath the Indian. He stared up into the tree as if he expected to see the same thing Two Bears saw through the scope. "What's happening? Can you tell?"

"One of the wagons has broken a wheel. Lavalle is shouting, but I can't make out what he's saying. That damned beard covers too much of his mouth for me to read his lips."

While Slocum paced restlessly under the tree, Two Bears continued to watch. Slocum stepped back to the horses, realizing they were going to be stopped for a while. He took both sets of reins and looped them around the trunk of a smaller tree. Slocum sat on the ground, his back against the small tree. The wind was picking up again, and he shrugged deeper into his borrowed jacket.

The first flakes were so delicate, he didn't realize what they were. Wiping at his cheek to chase away some fuzz, milkweed or a strand of spiderweb, he felt the water under his fingers. He looked up at the sky and saw the light snow swirling overhead, pale specks that seemed to melt just before reaching him.

The snow seemed to swell in intensity as he watched. The flakes grew larger, and soon they were sweeping past him in sheets, blown by gusts of wind. A soft hiss filled his ears as the icy flakes sifted through the leaves overhead. The ground around him was already beginning to collect a fine white dust. He scraped at it with his fingers, ignoring the cold. He picked up a broad leaf and shook it, watching the snow slide off and land in his lap.

He wondered whether the snow would be a blessing or a curse. Deciding it was a toss-up, there was nothing he could do except hope it was the former. They were already too much up against it to have to endure yet another impediment. Getting to his feet, he walked back to the larger tree and looked up into the leaves.

Slocum shook his head with closed eyes, trying to sharpen his vision. In the lowering darkness, Two Bears was only dimly visible among the brittle leaves. The Indian was still intent on his scrutiny of the halted wagons. He looked as if he had been carved out of wood or as if he were some strange outgrowth of the tree itself.

Walking back to the horses, Slocum patted his own pony, brushing snow from its mane. The horses seemed skittish, and he wondered if that meant the snow would be a bad one. It seemed early in the year for that to be a possibility, but not much had gone right for him since he'd entered Montana Territory. He saw no reason why nature shouldn't chip in with its own abuse.

The tree shook as Two Bears shinnied down its trunk. He still held the telescope in one hand.

Slocum waited until he had put it back in its leather case before asking his first question. "What's going on?"

"I think we finally got a break," Two Bears said. Slocum realized the Indian was almost smiling. "They're leaving the broken wagon behind."

Slocum interrupted. "How's that a break?"

"They're also leaving two men to work on it," the Indian finished.

"We wait until dark, then," Slocum said.

Two Bears nodded. The smile was gone. He had celebrated his good fortune; now the grim work of cashing it in had to be done. The Indian grabbed his pouch of dried meat and pulled out a handful. He offered the pouch to Slocum, who refused it. Getting to his feet, he walked to the horse and draped the pouch over the animal's back.

Two Bears ate in silence. Slocum lay on the cold ground and closed his eyes. He shivered as the snow sifted down his neck, then rolled over on his stomach, cradling his head on folded arms. It would be at least two hours before they had to move. Once they started, there was no telling how long before they'd get another chance to rest.

He could always eat on horseback if he had to, but sleep was confined to those few stationary moments, which were unpredictable in duration and frequency. Slocum wasn't hungry, but he was tired all the way through. So much had happened in so short a time, he could hardly believe it. And now, in just a few hours, the end of the long nightmare would commence.

Slocum dozed fitfully. The cold chewed at him, numbing his limbs and making his ears sting, but it was too much trouble to break out the bedroll, and he was just too damned tired. As he slept, strange images kept swirling through his mind. He wove them together with the aches in his body and the numbing cold.

Part of him knew that Two Bears would want to kill the two men who had stayed behind with the disabled wagon. Slocum didn't think it was necessary, so long as they were prevented from rejoining the others. Reducing the odds didn't require permanent removal. But he knew that tying them up and leaving them would condemn them to a slow death more cruel than outright murder.

He sorted through the nightmare images, desperately looking for some way to neutralize them, and each time he ran into a stone wall. He was a man in a deadly maze, only the death wasn't his own. Every corner he turned, two monstrous animals, men below the waist and grizzly above, confronted him. Each time, he sought to avoid conflict with them, but he was too slow to get around them, and too frail to overpower them. If he went after one beast, the other mauled him. If he turned on it, the first one clamped huge jaws over a knee, or slashed a shoulder with its claws.

He turned yet another corner and both beasts charged him at once. Each sank teeth into a shoulder, and they roared as they backed away, trying to tear him in two. He shouted in his sleep and sat up. It took him a moment to realize that Two Bears was shaking him. He wiped his eyes, sending a cascade of snow down his neck. He tried to rise, and only then noticed that he had been covered with a blanket.

Two Bears let go of him and stepped back. "There is more truth than we know in dreams," he said.

Slocum looked at him strangely. It almost seemed as if the Indian knew what he had been dreaming, and wanted to be certain he understood the warning.

"Let's go," the Indian said. He was already on his horse. As Slocum got to his feet, he saw the snow already covering the ground. Two or three inches crunched under his boots as he walked to his pony.

For half an hour, Slocum followed Two Bears through the heart of the valley. When the Indian stopped, Slocum knew the rest of their journey would be on foot. Two Bears slipped off his horse and unlashed the carbine dangling from its side. Slocum took his own rifle and followed the big Indian into the trees. Ahead, like an opening to another world, an orange hole shimmered in the darkness. The noise howled high overhead as it swept into the valley and down through the trees. The hiss of steadily falling snow crackled like flames in the dry leaves.

They found the wagon with no trouble. The huge fire sizzled off to one side as the snow drifted down into the flames and boiled away almost instantly. Huddled against the wagon, two men lay sleeping. Beyond them, a broken wheel, almost refitted, leaned against the wagon bed. Stacks of kegs stood three high beyond the wagon. They had had to unload in order to get the wheel off the ground for removal and repair.

Two Bears moved forward stealthily. Slocum followed him, staying to one side to keep the sleeping men in sight. The Indian got to the wagon and knelt beside the sleeping men. Slocum stood behind him. He saw the Indian reach out and clamp a hand over the first man's mouth. The sleeper tried to sit up, struggling against the pressure over his mouth. Two Bears moved his other hand as if to shake him. The man's eyes seemed to explode, then rolled back, leaving nothing but their whites showing.

The second man sat up as Two Bears started to rise. A sharp thud brought a bloody froth to the man's lips. In the firelight, it looked ghostly orange, and seemed to glow as it oozed down his chin. As Two Bears shifted his weight, Slocum saw the hilt of the Indian's knife sticking out of the man's chest. His hands were clasped awkwardly around its base, like the hands of a man in desperate trouble turning to prayer as his last resort. Blood trickled among the fingers as the man fell backward and lay still.

Only then did Slocum realize the first man, too, was dead. The snow on either side of him was cherry red where the blood from his slit throat drained into it, its heat melting the snow and turning it to ice. Now Slocum knew that his nightmare was no dream. Two Bears was bent on total destruction.

And he was surprised at how little he cared.

19

As morning dawned, Slocum stood on a heap of boulders. The snow continued to come down in turbulent swatches. As far as he could see in any direction, the ground was white, its contours blurred and softened by the accumulation. Two Bears sat silently, huddled in a blanket. They were too close to Lavalle to risk a fire, and Slocum envied Lavalle and his men the warmth of their own roaring blaze.

The caravan had holed up in a small box canyon. The three wagons were arrayed across the mouth of the canyon in a staggered arc. It had been difficult to map the layout in the dark. They had been unable to get too close, for fear their footprints might give them away. Two Bears had circled around behind the canyon, approaching it from above. The walls were almost sheer, nearly a hundred feet high, and the narrow mouth was the only way in.

The canyon was easily defended against a frontal assault, and no other approach was realistic. If it hadn't been for Amanda's presence, Slocum and Two Bears could have planted themselves high above and behind the barrier of wagons. If they had been interested merely in picking off Lavalle and his men, like fish in a barrel, it would have been a cinch. But with Amanda in one of the wagons, they didn't have that luxury. One way or another, they would have to get close enough to get inside the canyon, and quick enough to get out again, without risking Amanda's safety.

Two Bears, his hatred white hot, had argued for an immediate attack. Only with great difficulty had Slocum talked the Indian out of such a plan. They had nearly come to blows. Slocum wondered what kept the Indian from striking out on his own. But, for whatever reason, patience had prevailed. Two Bears had retreated into a silence as cold as the weather and as stony as the canyon they had to penetrate.

Slocum wore the telescope around his neck. Climbing down from the boulders, he walked toward the nearest stand of trees. The trunks and branches were icy. Choosing the sturdiest, Slocum chipped the ice away with the butt of his Colt. It flaked off like glass in rounded sheets. As he climbed into the tree, he watched the slender column of dark gray smoke that spiraled up from Lavalle's camp, barely visible through the swirling snow. It was less than a half mile away, but it might as well have been a thousand miles.

Slocum was frustrated and angry. Every hour Amanda was Lavalle's prisoner was an hour of vulnerability. He had no illusions about the bearded giant. Despite his veneer of reason, Lavalle was a cold-blooded killer. The girl had value to him, but in the scheme of things, she was insignificant. Lavalle would do nothing drastic to protect her from his men. And, sooner or later, one of them would get a notion to see what all the fuss was about. Slocum could only hope he got there first.

As Slocum settled into the tree, Two Bears threw off his blanket and stood up. He looked toward the smoke, dimly discernible against the gray sky. Quietly, he threw a blanket on his pony and mounted. Flapping his knees, he urged the pony toward Slocum's tree.

"What are you going to do?" Slocum asked. He dropped

from the tree, prepared to resume his argument against attacking the wagons.

"We need to know more of what we are up against."

"So?" Slocum waited for an explanation. When none was forthcoming, he asked again, "What are you going to do?"

"They sell whiskey. I am an Indian." Two Bears stopped abruptly, as if that explained everything.

Slocum shook his head in exasperation. "Stop being so damned mysterious. Tell me what you're up to."

"I am going to buy whiskey. Why else would a dumb redskin be out in this weather?"

Slocum shook his head slowly. "I understand. It might work. But be careful."

"I don't have to be careful. And it will work. When Lavalle and his kind look at me, they don't see Two Bears. They see a customer. All Indians are the same to them. They will not even see me. They will look right through me, to the beaver and otter pelts they want from me."

"And while you bargain, you'll get a good look."

"If I can, I will look for the girl. But I have to make sure they don't get suspicious. They will expect me to be cautious, and to bargain hard. But they will know that I am not interested in them or their possessions. If I can get them to bite, I might be able to lure a few of them away. You'll have to be ready."

As they spoke, the snow began to lift a little. The sky brightened, and the wind died down. Two Bears examined the sky closely. "It won't last long," he said.

Without another word, he wheeled his pony and moved off toward the canyon. Slocum stood quietly. It was several minutes before Two Bears vanished into the flurrying snow. The wind came back, this time in gusts instead of the steady howl. Small whirlwinds spiraled among the trees, sucking snow off the ground and dropping it yards away as they spun themselves out of existence.

Slocum broke their camp. He wanted to be ready to move at the first sound of trouble. Two Bears was no fool, and he wouldn't take any unnecessary chances. But Lavalle was no fool either. If he suspected Two Bears to be anything but a customer for his whiskey, he wouldn't hesitate to kill the Indian.

Two Bears rode toward the canyon, trying hard to swallow his anger. What he was about to do contradicted everything his father had taught him, everything he believed in. Lying was anathema, for any reason. If a man had to defeat an enemy by deceit, he didn't deserve to be victorious. Two Bears tried to console himself with the notion that he was fighting a white man's battle now, and that it was permissible to use the white man's ways. But he didn't believe it. He wondered about this man Slocum, and whether lying was his way. Or was he different? Was Slocum perhaps more like an Indian than either of them realized? But that, he decided, didn't matter either.

By the time he reached an opening through the steep valley leading to the box canyon, the sun had started to break through. Two Bears knew that more snow was on the way, and hoped it would hold off long enough to carry out his plan.

A lone sentry stood at the mouth of the canyon, a carbine cradled crosswise in his arms. The man didn't seem to realize he was there until Two Bears was almost on him. As he drew closer, he could see that the guard was squinting against the bright glare off the snow. He raised his hand in greeting, letting his pony slow to a walk. The sentry levered a shell into the chamber of his carbine and brought the gun around. The muzzle was pointed at the ground, but it was obvious the man was on edge. It wouldn't take much to push him over.

"Hold it right there, Injun. What're you lookin' for?"

Swallowing his last bit of pride, Two Bears answered in a caricatured patois. "**Me want** whiskey, buy whiskey. You sell?"

The man raised his chin a little, still suspicious, but he had taken the bait.

"What if I do?"

"Me buy this many barrels . . ." Two Bears held up both hands, palms out, and displayed all ten fingers. The words stuck in his throat, but he was trapped now. He had no alternative but to continue in the same rough dialect.

"Ten, hunh? You want ten barrels?"

"This many," Two Bears said, wiggling the fingers.

"Ten, that's what I said, you dumb redskin. That's ten. You got ten fingers, ain't you?"

"This many," Two Bears said again, wiggling the fingers more vigorously.

"All right, now, you just hold on." He turned over his shoulder and hollered toward the wagons. "Clyde, you best come on out here, Clyde. You got a customer." Turning back to Two Bears, he said, "My boss'll be here in a second. You just wait, now. Okay? You wait."

Two Bears moved closer to the mouth of the canyon, but the guard brought his gun up a notch and held up a hand. "Wait there, I said."

A moment later, a huge man with a full dark beard stepped between two of the wagons. Two Bears knew at once it was Clyde Lavalle. He felt the tension spark through his muscles like an electric current. He took a deep breath and tried to remain impassive.

"What the hell's goin' on, Ralphie?" Lavalle made no effort to conceal his contempt for both his own man and the visitor. He stared at Two Bears, his eyes flat and still in his head. Two Bears had seen such eyes before, but it had been a long time.

"Injun says he wants to buy some whiskey," Ralphie informed his boss. "Ten barrels."

Lavalle kept his eyes fixed on Two Bears. "How come he come to us? You ask him that?"

"Unh, no, I didn't." Ralphie turned to Two Bears. "How come you come to us?"

"Shut up, Ralphie," Lavalle barked. "Just shut up." He looked at the guard for an instant, but his eyes flicked away and back so quickly, it was as if they had never moved. To Two Bears, he said, "What makes you think I got whiskey to sell?"

"All white men sell whiskey," Two Bears said. He did his best to sound confused, as if Lavalle were contradicting common knowledge. "You sell whiskey . . . ?"

Lavalle was not so easily placated. "Who *told* you I sell whiskey? You know it's against the law to sell whiskey to redskins, don't you?"

Two Bears sensed Lavalle's suspicions getting the upper hand. He had to do something to regain control. "Give many skins for whiskey. Many skins."

Lavalle's ears pricked up. He smiled a tight smile, but his eyes didn't move. "What kind of skins?"

"All kind. Beaver, otter, marten. Others."

"Ermine? You got ermine skins to trade for the whiskey?"

"Ermine? What is ermine?"

Lavalle laughed. "Weasel, white weasel skins. You got any of those."

Two Bears nodded.

"Let's see some samples. You bring any skins with you?"

Two Bears turned to the back of his pony, where the skins he'd taken from Lone Calf's village dangled on a short cord. He jerked the skins loose and tossed the bundle at Lavalle's feet. The big man bent to retrieve the pelts but never took his eyes off Two Bears.

A second man came out from behind the wagon barricade. "What's the trouble, Clyde?" he asked.

"No trouble. Just go on back in."

"How come you talkin' to this redskin?"

"Martin, I said go on back. I'm talkin' business. Now git out of here."

"What kind of business?"

The question was aimed at Lavalle, but Two Bears answered it. "Buy whiskey. Buy whiskey with skins." He pointed to the string of pelts in Lavalle's hand.

Martin looked at the skins and laughed. "You can't buy much with a few little pelts like that, Injun."

"Samples," Two Bears said.

"Hell, Clyde. We don't have time to be meetin' with this redskin. We got to move on, while the snow's let up. It could come back anytime. Probably will, too. I think we ought to hurry."

"This fella says he wants to trade ermine skins for whiskey. I came here to sell whiskey, and that's what I aim to do. Now, you got a problem with that?"

"Hell, yes, I got a problem. That Slocum fella ain't gonna just walk away. We got a blizzard already half started, and we got a hostage might not make it to San Francisco in one piece. You want to piss it all away, go ahead. But I don't think we should."

"Look, we already lost the five hundred we were gonna get for Slocum. I got more whiskey than Jed can drink in fifty years just settin' there in them wagons, and we ain't likely to see too many more customers before the winter settles in. Now, I say we see what this fella has to offer before we move on. A little hard bargainin' and we just might salvage a bad trip."

Two Bears sensed the tension between the two men. It

squared with what Slocum had told him, but it didn't look as if there would be any way to exploit it. For the moment, Martin was gumming up the works, and Two Bears had to push him aside.

"Give back skins," he said.

"What for," Lavalle said, jerking his head back to the Indian. "I thought you wanted to buy whiskey."

Two Bears looked pointedly at Martin and shrugged. He held his hand out for the skins, and Lavalle stepped forward, broadening his smile. "Don't worry about him. He just likes to mouth off once in a while. But I'm the chief here. You want whiskey, and I'm gonna sell it to you. But I got to see them skins first."

"You come. Look."

Lavalle held up a dirty hand. "Hold on, now. I can't do that. I got to stay here and run things. That's what chiefs do, ain't it? But I'll tell you what I'll do. I'll send a few of my men with a wagon. They can look at the skins. If they're okay, they'll make a swap right there. How's that sound?"

Two Bears nodded. "Good."

Lavalle smiled. He stuck out a hamlike hand. Two Bears looked at the hand as if it were a strange animal. When he failed to grasp it, Lavalle dropped it to his side. "Okay, then. You wait here, will you?"

Two Bears turned his back on the canyon and tugged his horse to one side. When he turned back, Ralphie and Martin were still there. Both men watched him without speaking. A sudden clamor caught his attention. Two Bears turned to the mouth of the canyon again in time to see the wagon barricade shift. Lavalle was striding through the snow toward him.

Another wagon pulled between the two placed across the mouth of the canyon. Two men occupied the seat. The wagon rolled unsteadily, its wheels slipping on the snow as often as they turned. Lavalle stopped alongside his two men. In a hurried whisper, he exchanged words with Martin. When they were finished speaking, Ralphie cursed and ran toward the wagon. He climbed into the rear as it rolled past.

"Okay, Chief, take them to your village. Jed, the driver, has full authority to bargain with you. You got the goods, you get the whiskey. If not, not."

Two Bears nodded.

Lavalle ran after the wagon. "Jed, remember, pick up our tracks here. You know where we're headed."

Two Bears mounted his pony and urged it forward. The animal moved past the wagon and took the lead. He wanted to put a little distance between himself and the wagon to give himself a safety margin. He just hoped Slocum was ready.

The men in the wagon were talking among themselves, and Two Bears strained to hear what they were saying, but the creaking of the wagon bed and the sloppy hiss of the wheels in the snow drowned out their words. It started to snow again. One of the men in the wagon cursed, but Two Bears kept on. As long as he kept moving, they'd have to follow him. If he stopped, they'd have the chance to change their minds.

The pony's hoofprints were beginning to fill in, forcing Two Bears to check the path ahead. As the snow picked up, it would be harder to follow his own trail back to the small notch where Slocum was to be waiting. The ambush was going to be tricky. Lavalle was pulling out, but a gunshot would carry, even in the snow. Success depended on total surprise. If Lavalle's men thought they were hopelessly pinned, they'd give up. If they thought they had a chance, they might choose to fight.

Two Bears spotted the notch two hundred yards ahead. He looked for some sign of Slocum but saw nothing. He slowed a bit, letting the wagon pull a little closer to him. At fifty yards, he saw a small mound of snow on one side of the notch, probably knocked loose as Slocum took his position.

The men in the wagon were still talking among themselves. They seemed to be too annoyed with having been sent on what they regarded as a fool's errand to pay any attention to what was happening around them.

As he reached the notch, Two Bears kneed his pony into a trot. Behind him, one of the men shouted, "Hey, Chief, slow down!" The gap between rider and wagon widened a little more. Ralphie again hollered for Two Bears to wait. This time, he turned to wave at the men in the wagon. They waved back frantically, and he brought his pony to a halt. He turned the animal sideways and sawed at the reins to keep it steady.

The wagon rolled into the notch between the tall boulders. Two Bears nudged his horse to one side as the wagon drew closer. He backed still further as it came abreast of him. Jed yanked on the brake, and the wheels locked. The horses still tugged, and the wheels skidded for several yards on the icy ground before Jed got them under control.

"Anything wrong?" Jed asked.

Two Bears leaned forward, as if he couldn't hear. He urged his horse in closer. Jed repeated his question. "Anything wrong, Chief?"

"Not now," Slocum answered. He had appeared above and behind Jed on a pile of boulders. He worked the lever on his carbine as Two Bears brought his own gun out from under his jacket.

"Not a sound," Slocum warned. "If you think I won't shoot, you're wrong. Make me do it, and you'll be *dead* wrong."

"What the hell is this?" Jed demanded. He looked at

Two Bears, and it finally dawned on him. "You're in ca-
hoots, ain't you? Hey," he turned to look at the man above
and behind him. "It's Slocum. You sonofa—" He went for
his pistol. Two Bears slammed the muzzle of his carbine
into Jed's temple, knocking him off the seat.

"I shoot the next one," he snapped.

"Tie them up," Slocum said.

As Two Bears stepped toward the wagon, he said,
"We're fresh out of rope, Slocum. Sorry."

20

Slocum could still smell the blood. Every time he looked at Two Bears, his nostrils quivered, as if the air between them were tainted with the sickening odor. To Slocum, it brought back painful memories. Every gust of wind seemed to remind him of another time, another place. Death was the thread that bound the times and places together. Himself and Two Bears. Himself and Lavalle. It was as if men were not bound so much by blood as by its spilling. And the air was full of it.

Two Bears was getting reckless. Twice he had left Slocum behind to ride close to Lavalle's small caravan. And twice he had come back stony-faced, his body shaking like a man on the edge of delirium. Slocum had seen it before.

The wounded, beyond help, their own bodies turning on them, the fever frying their brains, reducing the bodies to shivering jelly—that was one version. The other form was just as deadly. It was the blood lust, the passion to kill making men shake with uncontrolled nervous energy raging to escape. And on reflection, he realized there was little difference between the killers and the victims. Both were prisoners, sealed behind the same invisible bars, as if the nerves had become a net in which they both thrashed about like landed salmon.

It unnerved Slocum to see his companion in that light. He had to depend on the Indian. He was almost helpless without him. Yet to cooperate with him, or to use him, was to share the contagion. But there was no other way. Amanda's life was at stake, and if Slocum couldn't set her free, no one would. Watching the wagons negotiate the mountain passes, so innocent, so neutral, their dull gray and bleached wood as bland as oatmeal, it was hard to believe that the man who drove them had engineered two separate slaughters in the past week. Slocum wondered if he would ever be able to explain to another person what it had been like.

He had met Lavalle, had spoken with him. The man was eccentric, certainly, but there was nothing in his demeanor to betray the casual brutality he was capable of. And yet two villages lay in ruins, their inhabitants now as dead and silent as the snow that swirled around them and stretched like a funereal pall as far as the eye could see. And beyond the edge of vision, it went on to the limit of the mind's eye. It stretched out on all sides like that infinite silence that the dead shared with the snow, and the blankness their eyes shared with the snow-covered mountains.

Slocum wondered how long Two Bears could contain himself. There was no question that the Indian's rage was justified. And Slocum wasn't interested in passing judgment on the man or his conduct. But he had a tactical problem, rooted in the difference between rescue and revenge. If he had any hope of restraining his ally, he knew he had better have a plan that made sense. It didn't have to be perfect, but it had to be workable, and it had to have a reasonable chance of success.

Certainty was out of the question, even for the kind of full-bore frontal assault that so bedazzled Two Bears. And the best vengeance, as Slocum knew only too well, was the one that left the avenger alive to savor it. Revenge was so personal a thing, no one, not even a blood relative, could revel in the destruction of Clyde Lavalle and his entourage the way Two Bears himself was certain to do.

And Slocum thought of Blue Lake. It had been several days since he had seen her. Somewhere far to the south-east, beyond the foothills, she must be wondering what had happened to her brother. For a moment, Slocum thought he could use her as a wedge, some way to budge Two Bears off dead center. But as he thought about it, he realized that Two Bears was too deeply rooted, perhaps even more deeply than a full-blooded Blackfoot, in the cultural ethics that demanded he exact retribution.

Despite his proud assertion of his Indianness, Two Bears was confused about who and what he was. A man at ease with himself would not try so hard to expunge half of his heritage. That meant that Two Bears would be reluc-tant, perhaps even adamant in refusing, to accept anything that smacked of accommodation with the white man's law.

As if Slocum didn't have enough problems.

The snow continued off and on, sometimes swirling in thick, opaque sheets that all but obscured the trail left by the wagons and everything farther away than ten yards. Driven by a howling wind, the icy flakes hissed through the frozen leaves and slashed at their exposed skins and tormented the ponies. The sleetlike particles bounced off their buckskin clothing with the steady rattle of rain on a tin roof. The sun all but disappeared, the sky pressed in on them, and everything, earth and sky alike, turned the leaden gray of late twilight.

At other times, the snow seemed to sift down like flour, almost silent, collecting on the ponies' manes like dust. Sticky and heavy, it clotted in the creases of their clothes and gathered on the limbs and leaves around them until its weight forced the branches to bend or be broken. The wind was softer, too, more like a distant humming than a fierce wail.

The ground continued to rise more and more sharply.

The ponies were laboring, and Slocum knew Lavalle's draft horses had to be suffering. It was harder and harder to keep up with them without getting too close. The snow was beginning to accumulate at such a rate that even Two Bears worried about his ability to follow them. The wheel tracks were broad and sloppy. Slush built up between the spokes and fell away in great clumps, splashing broad, shallow swaths on either side. But the wind was driving the snow with such fury that the craters filled in almost at once. By the time Slocum and Two Bears passed the same spots, there was little more than a shadowy depression to betray the wagons' passage.

There were signs that the wagons would soon be forced to stop altogether. Here and there, abrupt arcs swept to either side of the trail, evidence that the wagons were breaking loose and slipping out of control. Several times they found places where the wagons had narrowly missed slamming into a tree or a boulder. The steadily advancing grade increased the frequency of such near misses. It was just a matter of time before a near miss became a collision.

Slocum could no longer see much beyond Two Bears, who fell back closer and closer to him. It was beginning to get dark, and the trail was treacherous even for the sure-footed ponies. Two Bears held up a hand and waited for Slocum to come abreast of him.

"I think they're going to try to reach the crest of this ridge and stop."

"Why?"

"They won't be able to control the wagons on the way down. Even if the wheels lock, they can still slide. The horses will be useless. The wagons are just too heavy. The far side is just as steep. And I think I know where they're going to stop. Elk Pass is up there. It's narrow and just below the top of the ridge. At the far end there's an old mining camp. They'll probably hole up there, at least until morning. They'd be fools to try to push on in the dark."

"How well do you know the terrain?" Slocum asked.

"Well enough. Probably better than they do." There was no pride in his voice. The flat, neutral tone was appropriate to a statement of fact. "The problem is the far side. If they go left coming out of the pass, they have a long, rough ride downhill. If they go right, they head into Buffalo Run, a long, winding pass that circles around on itself. The Cheyenne used to chase buffalo through and pick choice bulls from the cliffs on either side. If they take the down-hill route, we'll have to hang way back. There's hardly any cover, and they could spot us miles away against the snow."

"That's if we wait until it stops. What if we take them tonight?"

Two Bears either didn't hear the question or he ignored it. "If they try Buffalo Run, we can't get at them. It's too tight, but it's probably blocked by snowdrifts, anyway."

"And what if we take them tonight?" Slocum repeated. "The odds are a lot better than they were. As far as we know, they can't get help from anybody else. Even if they were planning to hook up with other runners, there's no way they can be on schedule now. We have the time, and we have the chance. Why not take it?"

Two Bears sat motionless on the pony. He swept his eyes across the snow-covered wasteland behind Slocum, then turned to look at the faint signs of the wagons' passage. He chewed on his tongue for an eternity, then licked his lower lip. "Why not?" he said.

"I don't understand," Slocum said. "Before, you were all for riding in and ripping their heads off with your bare hands. Why the change?"

Two Bears shook his head. "I don't know. Maybe I've come around to your way of thinking. Maybe there's been enough innocent death already. Maybe saving the girl is more important than anything else."

"Even vengeance?" Slocum asked.

"Maybe even vengeance." Two Bears tugged on the hackamore and swung his pony in a tight arc. The animal skittered sideways, looking for comfortable footing. It nickered and bucked its head. Slocum stared into the near darkness to his left. The pony seemed to be frightened of something on the slope above them.

"What . . ."

"Quiet," Two Bears hissed. The Indian stared into the same near-darkness. He wrestled the pony back into line, patting its shoulder and leaning over to talk to it.

"What's going on?" Slocum whispered.

"Probably nothing," the Indian said. "Or maybe a puma. Food has to be a little scarce. Let's go." Two Bears urged his pony forward. The animal struggled through snow nearly knee deep. Slocum's pony had an easier time, following in its footsteps. Both men knew there was no way the wagons could continue in the heavy going.

Two Bears angled his pony off the trail, slowly ascending the slope parallel to it. "Wait here," he said over his shoulder. Slocum was puzzled, but by now nothing the Indian did could surprise him. Two Bears slipped off the pony and vanished into the trees, leaning forward against the slippery footing.

Slocum dismounted and secured his own horse, then struggled up the slope to tie the Indian's horse to a stunted pine covered with snow. After a half hour, he was beginning to worry. Restless, with his nerves rubbed raw by the constant stopping and starting, Slocum kicked at the snow, gradually flattening a broad square across the trail. A sudden swish behind on the slope spun him around, his hand going for the Colt Navy.

Snow cascaded toward him, picking up speed and bulk

as it hissed down the tree-studded wall of the narrow canyon. Slocum dove to one side, keeping his hand on the gun but unwilling to risk drawing until he came to rest. If he lost it in the snow, it might be gone for good. Rolling over and over, Slocum raced the snow slide for several yards before coming to rest against a heavy drift. He scrambled up, pulling the Colt at the same instant.

His eyes were full of snow, and the rough edge of the buckskin sleeve rubbed his lids raw as he tried to clear it away. A blob of shadow followed the snow down and came to rest near Slocum's pony. He recognized the Indian as he cocked the Colt.

"It's me," Two Bears said, his voice muffled by the snow filling Slocum's ears. He gradually took on shape as he strode toward Slocum. "Put these on," he said. "We're going to take a walk."

He tossed a pair of makeshift snowshoes at Slocum's feet. "It took longer than I thought to find what I needed."

Slocum bent to pick up the pair of broad ovals. Flexible pine branches, lashed with rawhide and slatted with thick slabs of bark, they were crude but looked serviceable. Slocum sat in the snow to tie them to his feet with strips of chewed leather. He realized that Two Bears had cut strips from the bottom of his jacket to get enough to lace the snowshoes on.

They felt awkward at first, but as he stepped into the snow to test them out, he was surprised at how stable a footing they afforded him. "What about the horses?" Slocum asked. "The cat . . ."

"Don't worry about it. Come on." Two Bears grabbed his carbine, and Slocum followed suit. The Indian set a backbreaking pace. It took Slocum a while to get the hang of the shoes, half walking and half skating, lifting his feet just enough to slide them forward. He had to fight the urge to bend his ankles, which would snag the shoes in the snow.

It was still snowing, but the wind had stopped, as if it had been frozen solid by the plunging temperature. They entered a steeply faced declivity that Slocum took to be Elk Pass. It was nearly a mile to the far end, and by the time they got there, light was already glowing in the windows of two ramshackle buildings tucked in under a sheer rock face.

Beyond the buildings, the ruins of a wooden sluice and two or three cabins, now roofless, were outlined against the darkness of the rock wall by the snow that clung to the rough wood of their sides. They crept along the rock face, trying to get close enough to see through the murky glass.

Between the two occupied cabins, two wagons, their teams unhitched, stood in a row, their tongues already half buried in snowdrifts. Lavalle had been here for some time, at least two or three hours, Slocum guessed.

"You check the small building, I'll check the larger," Two Bears whispered. "I'll meet you behind the wagons when I'm finished."

"Don't start anything without me," Slocum warned.

Two Bears said nothing. Even in the near-darkness, Slocum could see the play of bunched muscles as the Indian clenched his teeth. He wanted to say something, but knew Slocum knew what he would say, and knew it wouldn't matter. A moment later he was gone.

Slocum kept to the wall, feeling his way with one hand, the carbine in the other. The cabin wasn't as close to the wall as it had appeared from a distance. There was a good twenty feet between the back wall of the small building and the sheer rock face towering above it. The snow behind the building was deeper where the wind had stacked it against the wall. The sharp slope of the drifts made walking awkward, even in the snowshoes, until Slocum started to crabwalk, leaning toward the wall to keep his balance.

An orange-gray block of light smeared the rock face. Slocum slipped forward, allowing himself to fall on his rump in the snow just inches from the back wall of the cabin. When he regained his feet, he crept along the wall until he could see the window. The drifts were so deep, he had to kneel to look into the room.

Slocum bent close to the glass, but it was difficult to see. He rubbed a gloved hand against the glass, but it didn't help much. Moisture from inside had frozen against the pane, covering it with a mossy, translucent ice that had spread like a lichen and glittered at its edges.

He wanted to open the window, but had no idea who might be inside. Slocum bent close to the glass and breathed fully on it, huffing and exhaling. The warmth of his breath started to melt the ice just enough to turn it into a small transparent circle an inch or so across. He bent to the glass, wiped the ice of his own breath from the outside, and peered through. On a narrow cot, a thin blanket draped around her like a child's favorite outgrown quilt, Amanda Dawson shivered.

As near as he could tell, she was alone. He tapped on the glass, but she seemed not to hear him. A small bruise discolored one cheek, but she seemed otherwise unharmed. He tried the window, but it was sashless. He listened for a moment, and heard nothing but a low, sobbing wind moaning around the corner of the cabin. He slipped his feet out of the snowshoes, placed one heel at the center of one pane, and pushed. The rotten wood molding gave way, and the glass opened as if hinged. It hung for a long moment, and Slocum scrambled to grab it before it could fall free and shatter.

Amanda heard the squeal of glass and wood and looked toward the window. The dim light wasn't enough to illuminate Slocum's face, and Amanda seemed to shrink away from the window, but she was unwilling to run to her captors for protection.

Using a knife, Slocum peeled the rest of the glass away, then yanked the rotten wood crossbars from the frame. He slipped through and landed with a thud. Amanda stared at him for a long time, her mouth gaping, lips quivering. She raised one hand to her mouth. Her eyes looked too big for her face by half.

Slocum crossed the room on tiptoe. He knelt by her side just as recognition seemed to dawn.

"Mr. Slocum, it's you, isn't it?" she asked. She seemed more confused than surprised.

He nodded, and held a finger to his lips. "Ssshh. Just do what I tell you and—" A sudden shout from outside the room brought him up short.

In a voice half muffled by the rotting wood walls and half blurred by obvious inebriation, someone mumbled with the loud belligerence of a drunk. "Damnit, Joe, I'm tellin' you I'm gonna see she *is* a virgin, that's damn all I'm gonna do. Can't sell her nohow, she ain't."

"Martin, you crazy man, Lavalle will cut your balls off."

"Sall right wimme, Joeyboy. He needs 'em, you ask me. Course you don't tell him, he ain't gonna know nothin', is 'e?"

"I won't say nothin, I swear it, Martin."

"Then don't worry 'bout it. I'll just slip on in there and see just how virgin the li'l gal might be. Don't nobody have to know she is or she ain't. 'Cept me." He laughed drunkenly, and they heard his hand rattle the latch.

Joey mumbled something as he moved off.

Slocum held a finger to his lips and pressed himself against the wall behind the door. He shifted his knife from hand to hand, trying to find a comfortable grip. Amanda, her eyes even wider now, stared at him, and he waved her gaze off, trying to signal her to look somewhere else. The door banged open, and Martin tripped to the floor on his way in.

He fumbled with his fly as he tried to get up. He kept calling in a drunken monotone, "Mandy. Woohoo, Mandy. Doctor's here. Woohoo, Mandy." Martin rolled onto his back, laughing drunkenly. He belched, and a small drool of regurgitated whiskey ran down his chin. He got his fly open and turned around, his head wobbling as he got to his knees. He called to Mandy, getting one foot on the floor, then laughed again. He seemed unable to rise.

Martin stopped in midair, as if he sensed something, and turned toward the open doorway. Slocum held his breath as Martin finally managed to get to his feet. Talking to himself, the drunken man stumbled back to the doorway and slammed the flimsy door closed. He seemed to realize Slocum was there at the same instant. He went for his gun as Slocum stepped forward, the knife extended in one hand. It bounced off a rib, then slid home.

Martin's eyebrows collapsed over his eyes, which blinked twice, then clouded up. He looked like a man who has just realized he left his wallet on the bar. His head still wobbling drunkenly, Martin took a step back, pulling himself off the blade and covering his gut with both hands. His mouth opened, and a single bubble of blood expanded as his jaw sagged. Its surface reflected the lamp like a soap bubble before it burst.

Slocum grabbed Amanda and hauled her to her feet. Wrapping her tightly in the blanket, he pushed her through the window out into the snow. A tattered woolen coat hung on a hook by the door, and he grabbed it and stuffed it through after the girl.

It was almost over. But not just yet.

21

"You wait right here, Mandy. It's almost over."

"I want to go home."

Slocum wrapped the blanket around her a little tighter. "I know you do," he said. "And you're going to. Just hold on a little longer."

Slocum padded over the snow, his snowshoes hissing on the thick drifts. He looked back once, and was satisfied. Amanda was almost invisible, tucked away under the trees.

When he reached the wagons, Two Bears was already there. The Indian waited for him to speak first.

"She's safe," Slocum said. "I got her, and she's safe."

"No she's not. She won't be safe until Lavalle is dead. And I think you know that."

"Hasn't there been enough killing already?"

"I don't know. You tell me. Was it enough when they killed my mother? Was it enough when they killed Lone Calf? Was it enough when *you* killed Martin? How much is enough? When all the Indians are dead? When all the bad guys are dead?"

Slocum had no answer. He doubted if there was one. But he knew Two Bears was right. Lavalle would never walk away from this, not now. He had too much invested. And, for whatever distorted reasons, he almost certainly would believe he was entitled to exact vengeance.

"All right," Slocum said. "What do you want to do?"

"Do? I want to go fishing in the spring. That's what I want to do. The real question is what do I have to do to make sure I have the chance."

"Don't play word games with me, Two Bears." Slocum turned his back on the Indian, frustrated at his own inability to control events. Things were getting out of control now, and there was nothing he could do but swim with the current and try to keep his head above water.

Slocum felt a hand on his shoulder, surprisingly gentle. "Look, Slocum, I know you think this is easy for me. But it isn't. And nothing you can say or do will change that. Lavalle isn't even a man to me. He's an animal, a mad animal. And you have to do with him what you would do with a mad dog. You destroy him. There is no other way. None."

Slocum shook his head slowly. "I know that. I just wish—"

"Save your wishes. There's nothing you could wish for here."

The two men shook hands. They searched the wagons for anything useful. Two Bears came up with Wilbur Hartley's buffalo gun and a leather pouch full of ammunition for it. He gave the gun to Slocum, then doused the wagons in whiskey, as he had the others. Slocum kept watch on the cabin. He moved to the horses and waited for the sign from Two Bears.

When the big Indian waved, Slocum cut the horses loose. He didn't bother to chase them off, knowing the explosion would take care of that. A moment later, the first flicker peeped out from a corner of one of the wagons. The flames spread quickly, and Two Bears ignited the second wagon. When he was satisfied they'd caught, he flatfooted it to Slocum's position. They lay in the snow, their weapons trained on the cabin door.

"Come on, damn it," Slocum whispered. "Blow!"

Thick smoke coiled up into the snowy air. Whipped by the wind, it trailed off into black tatters before it cleared the rocky face behind the burning wagons.

And then the first barrel blew, ripping the canvas top of the wagon to flaming shreds. They spun crazily in the air, trailing sparks from their blazing edges. The wagonload of whiskey kegs, some ruptured by the blast, flew in every direction. One keg spun high into the air trailing a small plume of fire. It slammed into the cliff face far above the wagon bed, shattering on impact and drenching the stone wall with a cascade of shimmering blue light.

Some of the kegs rolled, their split seams spewing cheap whiskey in whirling fountains of fire. The booze arced through the snow, then quickly sputtered out as it melted the snow beneath it and extinguished itself in the meltwater.

The cabin door banged open, and a figure stood for a moment, outlined against the lamplight from the room behind him. Slocum recognized Hartley almost immediately. Hartley leaped into the snow. He hit on one shoulder and rolled over twice before getting to his feet.

Hartley raced toward the second wagon, and Slocum realized he was running for the Sharps. Slocum sighted in slowly, patiently, as Hartley floundered through the hampering drifts. Hartley fell once, his arms flailing like a drowning man in deep water. Slocum squeezed the trigger, and the big Sharps slammed into his shoulder. Hartley went down again, and this time lay still. He looked no more substantial than a dark shadow on the snow.

A second man darted through the door. Smarter than Hartley, he dove into the darkness alongside the cabin. Slocum watched, screwing his eyes into a squint, waiting for the first sign of movement. When none came, Two Bears whispered to him. "I'm going to get closer."

Slocum, his eyes still pinned to the cabin wall, felt

rather than saw Two Bears back away. A sudden scurry at the base of the cabin caught his eye. Slocum squeezed his eyes still tighter, trying to pierce the darkness by desire. He noticed a mottled clump of shadow that could have been a man or snow on a stack of firewood. He sighted in and squeezed. The big buffalo gun bucked, its report bouncing off the rocky walls a dozen times before fading away.

A bright muzzle flash, to the left of where he had aimed, was followed by the crack of a rifle. Slocum's cold fingers fumbled with the next cartridge for the single-shot buffalo gun. Whoever lay in the snow at the base of the cabin wall wasn't so hampered. A second report, then a third, barked at him. The third shot came close, slamming into the thick trunk of a lodgepole pine a few feet behind him.

The cartridge slid home with a click, and he swung the Sharps around. A distant rumble, like a far-off herd of cattle in sudden flight, caught his ear. The rumbling grew louder and exploded with an ear-shattering blast as the second wagon blew apart.

A great white cloud mushroomed away from the rocky wall, and Slocum's hands and cheeks were stung in two dozen places. He shook his hands in pain, bringing them close to examine them. Hard white welts stippled his hands. With trembling fingers, he felt the same small, hard knots on his cheeks and forehead. The skin hadn't been broken, and there was no sign of blood.

Puzzled, he looked back at the cloud for several seconds before it dawned on him. He dug in the snow around him until he found what he was looking for. Lavalle's supplies had been in the second wagon. The cloud of flour was painless, but the dried beans had stung like hornets.

There was less whiskey in the second wagon, but it had scattered burning debris in every direction. One keg had smashed into the roof of the cabin, spilling liquid fire across the roof as it splintered. The whiskey ran down the cedar shakes and splashed the wall with pale blue flames. In the eerie light, Slocum could see more clearly.

The hidden rifleman fired again, and this time Slocum was ready. The muzzle flash had marked his location, and the ghostly blue light of the burning whiskey etched him starkly against the wall like a figure on an architect's drawing. Slocum steadied his hands, and the Sharps exploded a third time. The huddled shadow seemed to implode, leaving little more than a dark stain behind on the snow.

The roaring flames drowned out most other sound. Slocum heard a crash that sounded like breaking glass. He scanned the area on either side of the cabin, but there was no sign of Two Bears. Cramming another shell into the Sharps, Slocum scrambled to his feet. He slung the buffalo gun over his shoulder and started toward the cabin. A figure in the cabin doorway opened up, but it was too small to be Lavalle. Slocum held his revolver in his left hand and fired twice at the doorway. The shadowy figure ducked back, then reappeared, sprawled on the floor.

Two more shots whined past Slocum as he slogged through the snow. The snowshoes made walking possible, but they slowed him up, and he was forced into a crouch. A slight movement to his right brought him up short, and he dove headlong into the drifts. After wiping the snow from his eyes, he checked the muzzle of his gun to make sure it wasn't clogged.

The movement had crystallized now, and he recognized Two Bears. The Indian had reached the corner of the cabin and dropped to his knees. Slocum fired once more, this time taking time to aim carefully. He saw a chunk of wood split off the doorway, and the man on the floor rolled away from the opening.

Two Bears was just six feet from the open door, and Slocum had to hold his fire. He climbed to his feet again.

orking off to the right to get a better angle on the gun-
man. He saw nothing. Suddenly, the light in the cabin went
out. Slocum cursed and started forward, keeping his
crouch as low as the snowshoes would allow.

Two Bears was just outside the door, pressed flat
against the wall. The Indian waved one hand high overhead, and Slocum charged forward. The roof of the cabin
continued to burn, and as Slocum drew close, a high slab
of blue flame collapsed into the cabin, spilling its light into
the building. By the garish blue illumination, Slocum
could still see no one inside.

Two Bears spun and stepped into the cabin as Slocum
closed on the doorway. There was a cluster of gunshots,
but Slocum couldn't tell who had fired. Two Bears spun to
the right, and Slocum thought he might have been hit. He
charged through the doorway and dove to the floor. Skid-
ing on one shoulder, he slammed into a rude wooden
table, scrambling to get to his feet even before he stopped
sliding. One of the snowshoes snapped free. Slocum
kicked the other one loose.

Two Bears held a scrawny man by the shirtfront, a pistol at the man's chin.

Slocum hollered, "Don't!" He hauled himself up and
rushed toward the Indian, pushing the pistol aside to step in
between him and his captive.

Slocum grabbed the man by his shirt and realized it was
soaked with blood. In the blue-tinted light, it looked like
wet tar. "Where's Lavalle?" Slocum shook him. The man
was nearly unconscious. His head wobbled drunkenly.
"Where is he?" Slocum shouted.

The man sagged to the floor, and Slocum let go of the
shirt. He looked at his hands, stained and sticky with
blood, and wiped them on his pants.

"There." Two Bears was pointing.

Slocum saw the smashed window in the rear wall of the

cabin. He ran toward the ruined window, stumbling ove
the end of a burning beam. He lost his balance and fell t
his knees, just catching himself on the jagged wood of th
wrecked window before slamming into the wall.

The cabin shuddered. A groaning sound began far away
its pitch so deep it shook the floor. It raced nearer, th
rumble of a runaway freight, and the floor trembled like
frightened puppy.

"Get out!" Two Bears shouted. His words were almos
drowned out by the sound of rending wood. Slocum turne
to see a huge beam crash to the floor. The color of the ligh
was changing as the alcohol burned away. The wood wa
old and dry, and it was burning on its own now, a savag
yellow slashing across the doorway like swords in sunlight

Two Bears backed toward the door. Slocum started afte
him, but another beam creaked and started to fall. Slocur
spun around and hauled himself out through the broke
window. He fell into a deep drift just as the rest of the roo
collapsed behind him. He could feel the ground shake eve
through the snow as the heavy timbers fell to the floor o
the building.

The Sharps was still slung over his shoulder. He yanke
it free before turning to look back through the window
Two Bears stood beyond the doorway, and he waved whe
he saw Slocum's face reappear. The Indian shouted some
thing, but Slocum could hear nothing over the roarin
blaze.

The whole scene was alive with yellow and orang
light. Several of the ruined buildings had caught fire, an
Slocum could see Lavalle's footprints clearly. He plunge
after the bearded giant, struggling with the thick clots o
snow that kept clinging to his boots. As he left the holo
caust behind, Slocum could hear the wind howling hig
overhead.

Two hundred yards past the sluiceway, itself beginnin

o burn, the flames chewing their way up the steep face of
he mountain, the slope flattened enough to permit a man
o climb it. Lavalle's tracks swerved to the right at a forty-
ive-degree angle. The big man was working uphill and
way from the ruined camp below. Slocum was able to see
Lavalle's head and back as he climbed over a clump of
boulders, then he disappeared again.

Away from the protection of the steep walls of Elk Pass,
he wind was more aggressive. It ripped at Slocum's
lothes, slashing his face with frozen snow. Slocum
topped to call to Lavalle. He cupped his hands and
houted, but the words were hurled sideways by the wind.
Slocum didn't even hear his own voice.

He knew he was shouting only by the raw fire in his
hroat.

Slocum knew he was backlit by the blazing ruins below.
But he also knew that Lavalle, once he got over the ridge
nd into the pine forest on the other side, was gone for
ood. It was tempting to be cautious, to pick his way care-
ully through the clumped shrubbery and jumbled rocks.
Everything was buried under mounds of snow, and La-
alle's tracks were obvious. The big man cared more about
etting away than concealing his route.

But caution was not on Slocum's mind. He could think
nly of Lavalle and how much he wanted him, dead or
live; it made no difference. He realized that he was com-
ng ever closer to Two Bears' way of thinking. And the
ealization made him smile.

Without the snowshoes, Slocum could make no real
me. Lavalle had the edge. At any moment he could de-
ide to turn around and wait for Slocum, behind a tree, in a
epression between drifts, crammed in between boulders,
Lavalle could take his pick. As the flames behind him rose,
Slocum saw his shadow, a grotesque blue smear on the
now, and he knew what he had to do.

Once Lavalle passed over the top of the hill, he would be in darkness. Slocum dropped to his stomach and brought the Sharps around. He made sure there was a cartridge in the chamber, then he waited. He knew that every second he allowed Lavalle to lengthen his lead was a second he couldn't make up. But he also knew that Lavalle could not outrun the Sharps, not as long as Slocum could see him.

The waiting seemed interminable, even though it had only been a few minutes. So far, the flickering orange light continued to grow. It was as if the light, too, wanted to keep pace with Lavalle. But the wreckage wouldn't burn forever. And Slocum rubbed his eyes. He was exhausted and the gun was unfamiliar. He would get only one shot, and it damn well better be a good one.

Then, as if in answer to a prayer he had not yet offered, Lavalle's lumbering bulk rose up out of a gentle depression in the mountainside. A clump of pines stood to his left, but there was nothing between him and his stalker.

Slocum spotted Lavalle immediately. He had to estimate the range, and he was conscious of the swirling wind. Lavalle floundered, as if he were trying to avoid something directly ahead of him. He swerved to the right, moving farther away from the cover of the pines. The wind snarled once, then held its breath.

Slocum didn't even hear the gun go off. Intent on Lavalle, he only knew he'd fired when Lavalle threw his arms high over his head. Slocum thought he'd scored, but Lavalle turned to one side. He began to move his legs and pump his arms, but his progress was painfully slow. Slocum was struggling to get another round into the breech. When it slid home and he locked it in, he heard the noise.

Lavalle seemed to be nailed to the spot. His legs jerked up and down, and his arms swirled as if he were swimming. Then Slocum knew why. The leading edge of the snow suddenly roared into view, like a great wave about to crash on the beach. Triggered by the report of the Sharps, the avalanche hurled great swirls of snow high overhead, like the spume of a cresting breaker.

The slide followed the contours of the mountain, taking the path of least resistance. Slocum struggled to his right as the snow thundered down, snapping the smaller trees with a sound like artillery fire. He threw the Sharps away to lose its weight. Over his shoulder, he saw the advancing snow veer to the left, sliding down a V-shaped gully in the side of the mountain. The front end of the avalanche was littered with fractured timber and small boulders. One edge of the slide plowed through a stand of sturdy pines, leaving assorted debris behind.

Slocum was winded. He glanced at the sky for a moment, as if in thanks, then looked at the burning wreckage below. Starkly outlined by the orange light, wrapped in greasy smoke, Two Bears and Amanda Dawson hugged each other and stared up the mountain. Slocum sat down to catch his breath. The rumble of the snow died away, and he wanted to shout that he was all right, but the wind made it futile.

Angling toward the edge of the snow's path, Slocum stepped into the pines. Broken tree limbs were stacked like flood wreckage, jutting out at all angles from the mounded snow. As he skirted the edge and stepped onto the clear ground, all but stripped of its own snow cover, something caught his eye. He moved closer in the uncertain light from the fire.

Bending low to be sure, Slocum nodded silently to himself. He was certain now that it was over. Tangled among the litter, nearly wrapped around the trunk of a lodgepole, as broken as the limbs surrounding it, lay the battered corpse of Clyde Lavalle.

Epilogue

Slocum slid into bed quietly. He lay back on the cool, clean sheets and pulled a blanket to his waist. The window was halfway open, and he let the cold air play across his skin. It was snowing lightly, and a few flakes puffed in every time the curtain blew back.

The room was dark, but a block of light marked the doorway to the rest of the house. He could hear Lynn Dawson in the bath, the water lapping against the tub as she stood. The long, slow drip as she rose to climb out faded away. He closed his eyes, listening to the soft rasp of the towel on her skin.

He heard her feet on the wooden floor and opened his eyes. She had turned the lamp down, and her figure was soft and full against the dim light behind her.

"Bring the lamp," he said.

She laughed. "Why, did you forget what I look like?"

"Uh-uh. I remember. That's *why* I want you to bring the lamp."

"You flatter me, sir."

"I mean to."

"Is that all?"

"Bring the lamp, and find out."

When she turned, she stood for a moment with one hand raised, resting on the doorframe. The pose accented her breasts, as she knew it would. Slocum waited a long moment, then he whistled.

"*Now* I'll get the lamp," she said.

She was back a moment later, her bare feet shuffling on the floor. She held the lamp carefully, waist high. It looked almost as if she meant to hide behind it, but the light had the opposite effect. Highlighting her breasts and the tangled curls between her thighs, still damp from the bath, she succeeded only in calling attention to the lushness of her body.

"Recognize me?" she asked.

"I think we've met before," he said. "But I'm not sure. I think further confirmation is called for."

"With the light on?"

"As I recall, you once took off your clothes in broad daylight, in the great outdoors, no less."

"That was different. That was a picnic." She set the lamp on a small table next to the bed.

"So is this," Slocum said, reaching for her. His hand found her hip, and he pulled her gently down. She lay on top of the blanket, stretching her arms above her head. Slocum rolled onto his side and kissed her. She opened her mouth, but held the pose. He laughed, then slid his mouth to the hollow of her throat. He worked his way down slowly, pausing every now and then to look at her face. Lynn's eyes were closed.

"I think you're ignoring me," he said.

She ignored that, too. He stopped at her navel, slipping his tongue in for a second, the moved on. When he got to her bush, he tugged a few curls between his teeth. A glance upward showed her eyes were still closed. He moved still lower, starting down one thigh. Her legs parted, with agonizing slowness. By the time he reached the knee, they were wide open. He started back up, this time on the inside of her thigh. The bath oil made her skin slippery under his tongue, but its taste was not unpleasant.

Brushing the damp moss with his lips, he switched to the other thigh and started down toward the knee again.

"You seem to have missed something," she whispered.

This time, Slocum ignored her.

At the knee, he started back, even more slowly. When he reached the curls again, he paused for several seconds. Her thighs tightened, and she arched upward a bit. Slocum smiled to himself but said nothing. He darted his tongue into the tangles, finding the heart of her with its tip. Teasingly, he traced the thick lips with his tongue, backing away as her hips rose still higher. She moaned, wriggling her ass as she tried to tempt him deeper into the jungle.

When he could stand it no longer, he plunged all the way in, his tongue darting wildly, lapping the musky juice and probing deep inside her.

"*Now* you've got my attention," she said.

"I intend to keep it for a while, too," he said.

He crawled between her thighs. He was so hard it hurt. She reached for him, found his shaft, and guided him home. As he slid in, savoring the long, deliberately slow penetration, she wrapped her arms around his back. Her hands pressed on his hips, pulling him deeper.

He felt her lips close to his ear, then the hot breath. She whispered, "I know this is the last time. Don't worry about it."

He started to disagree, but she stopped him with a squeeze. "It is, and I think it's best. Let's just make this a night neither of us will regret . . . or forget."

Slocum started a steady, rocking rhythm. He closed his eyes and thought about the last few days. The warmth of Lynn's body drained away the last of his anger. As he continued to ride her, he felt the rage well up in him.

Lynn, as if she sensed it, urged him on, driving him faster and faster. She curled her long legs around him, beating time with her heels on the backs of his thighs. Her short, sharp cries grew louder, their rhythm faster. Cresting together, she buried her face in his shoulder, with a long, low groan somewhere between pleasure and pain. As he started to pull back, she held him for a second, then, as if changing her mind, pushed gently on his hips.

Lynn climbed to her knees as he lay back on the bed. She bent to kiss him on the forehead. "Thanks," she whispered. "Good-bye, I won't see you in the morning."

Slocum nodded. "I understand. Good-bye, Lynn."

Then she was gone. It was over. It saddened him, for reasons he understood only dimly, and that she would understand not at all. But he couldn't stay, and she wouldn't have it any other way.

But there was, after all, still the rest of his life to be lived. He had miles to go. And Blue Lake had promises to keep.

JAKE LOGAN
TODAY'S HOTTEST ACTION
WESTERN!